EXTREME ROAD RAGE

By

ANTHONY BOLTON

To my wife Jean for all her patience and support whilst I was writing this book and for her rigorous proof reading.

Copyright 2011 © Anthony Edward Bolton
ISBN No. 978-1-4478-1489-4

CHAPTER ONE

The picture on the screen was one of total devastation. Norman Parker sat watching the scenes being relayed from the M6 motorway with absolute revulsion. Normally a mild mannered man, Norman was shaking with uncontrollable anger. When would it ever end. The newscast had brought it all back again.

He was back in the car again on that lovely summer day five years ago when he and his wife Jenny had decided to take their two small daughters on a visit Chester Zoo. It was perfect. The sun was shining, the sandwiches were packed in the boot along with a push chair for the youngest one and they were doing a steady fifty five along the inside lane. Jenny was singing nursery rhymes along with the children who were strapped securely into their baby seats.

The first inkling of impending disaster Norman had was on looking in his rear view mirror to see the whole back window of the car filled with the mirror image of the word VOLVO. Christ he thought. Where the hell did he come from? There had been nothing even close to him the last time he had checked only a couple of minutes earlier. He suddenly became aware of headlights flashing and the blaring of a dual-tone horn above the sound of the nursery rhymes.

The next thing he remembered was wakening up in bed being slightly dazzled by intense white light. Everything seemed white. He tried to sit up but he was restrained by a cool, gentle hand holding firmly down by the shoulder.

Slowly he became aware of tubes and wires attached to various parts of his body and after a while he became aware of his surroundings. He was in hospital. He tried to shout out but it was only a hoarse whisper which emerged.

'Where's Jenny, where are the kids?'

He struggled to sit up again but the hand was still there pushing him gently back into the pillow. He never felt the needle go into his arm but was aware of a feeling of slipping very slowly off the edge of the bed and into oblivion.

It was two days before the doctor had judged that he could give him the devastating news that he had been the sole survivor of an accident involving his blue Ford Escort and a foreign heavy goods vehicle. Norman had passed out again, his brain automatically shutting his body down in an attempt to block out the agony of what he had been told.

Apparently no other vehicles had been involved in the accident. The foreign lorry had careered out of control due to a variety of faults in its braking and steering systems. They had been on the long, downhill section of the M6 approaching the Junction 26, the turn off for Skelmersdale when the truck driver had lost control and smashed into the back of the Escort causing both vehicles to plunge down the embankment. The sheer weight of the lorry had taken both vehicles through the "Armcor" barrier like a knife through butter. A length of wooden fencing post had sliced through the car like a rapier impaling his wife Jenny and their eldest daughter Natalie who was four years old.

Their six month old baby had, by one of those terrible quirks of fate, been struck on the head by another large splinter which had killed her outright.

Norman had received substantial crush injuries to his legs and abdomen together with a severe case of whiplash. Foolishly, as it turned out, he had removed the head restraints when he had bought the car, arguing that they restricted his view of the back seats when the children were aboard.

Two days on and still in hospital all he could feel was a terrible rage. It was tearing away at his insides like a steel claw. His own injuries had been fairly light considering the impact the car had sustained and at that moment in time, all he could think was why the hell had he not been killed as well. There was absolutely no point to life now without Jenny and the kids. They *were* his life.

The months that followed had been an absolute nightmare. The sight of those two tiny, white coffins beside that of his wife's had been almost too much to bear. How on earth he had got through the funeral service he would never know. He had, of course, been drugged up to the eyeballs with strong sedatives and was only vaguely aware of the kind words of sympathy and the usual platitudes. All the words in the world could never erase his complete feeling of desolation.

Six months after the funeral Norman had sold the family house for slightly less than the market value in order to get rid of it quickly. He could afford to do that, property prices having risen sharply since they had bought the house several years before. Besides, there were far too many memories there. Everywhere he looked he could see and hear Jenny chattering and children playing. He simply had to get away and try to make a fresh start. He had rented a small flat in the town centre close to his place of work. . . the work that had to a great extent helped him maintain some degree of sanity. He had thrown himself into his job often working late into the evening and most weekends. He couldn't bring himself to enjoy any sort of social life yet.

The television cameras were now zooming in on a baby's car seat which was laying on the hard shoulder. The image shook Norman out of his reverie and something snapped inside him. He picked up the heavy glass ashtray from the coffee table and hurled it through the screen.

In that explosive moment a terrifying idea entered his head. It was an idea so preposterous that he could feel the hairs on the back of his neck standing erect. He sat there for several minutes considering the magnitude of what he had thought. The thought was that he, Norman Parker, would bring about a radical change in the nation's transport policy. He would rid the country's roads of the thousands of heavy Juggernauts and get the freight back on the railways where it belonged. It was an outrageous concept and pretty frightening, but he was suddenly fired with great enthusiasm. He had once read that any goal could be achieved if the planning was meticulous and if the task was approached one small step at a time.

He sat there and considered that the majority of motorway accidents involved one or more heavy goods vehicles. They were too big, too heavy and too fast and they pounded the hell out of the road surfaces. If the roads were used by private cars and light commercial vehicles the motorways and main trunk routes would last far longer without the need for expensive re surfacing and maintenance. The money saved on all this work could be channelled into improving the country's railway infrastructure. It had angered Norman for years, the way the rest of Europe made use of their railways. They had invested in their rail networks over the years and had made good use of the trains for moving vast amounts of freight. Meanwhile in Britain the railway network had been decimated since Thatcher who admitted that, she personally, hated railways and so we all had to suffer. Once we had boasted the finest railways in the world but now they were run down and carried scarcely any freight at all. Of course Margaret Thatcher wasn't entirely to blame. There had been that maniac Beeching back in the fifties. Who the hell had let a bloody accountant loose on such a brilliant net-work. However, no use brooding on the past. The first priority was to form a plan of action.

Norman felt more alive at that moment than he had done since the accident. Once again he felt that he had something to live for. He had an aim in life once more. He would avenge his family's untimely death and perhaps, at the same time, purge some of the guilt that he felt at having survived when they had perished.

CHAPTER TWO

Norman went into the office the following day and booked two weeks holiday. His colleagues noticed a subtle change in him. Was it the slight bounce in his step, something in his eyes, a light to replace the deadness that had been there for the past few years?

Whatever it was they were really pleased. Perhaps he had found someone new in his life; most of the girls in the office eagerly subscribed to that theory. Most of the men hoped so too, but were less optimistic. Norman had completely withdrawn into some private hell after the accident. It was hardly surprising of course. None of them could imagine the agony which such a tragedy could cause and most of them had thanked God that it wasn't they who had suffered such a loss.

It was perhaps as well that they didn't know what had really caused this change. He needed the holiday to get down to some detailed planning. This would entail driving around the

Motorway network, something he didn't relish but it would have to be done. Friday evening came round quickly and after work he joined some of his work mates for a drink before returning home for a light evening meal. It was the first time he had done that since the accident and he had felt a little awkward at first. He realised that the social skills that he had always taken for granted had been eroded as a result of his self-imposed isolation.

The following morning he checked the oil, water and tyres on the car and threw a holdall into the back of the car. Having served a couple of years in the forces during National Service he was quite used to travelling light. He smiled sadly as he remembered how Jenny had always packed for him when they went away on holiday. There was always twice or three times as much as he needed stuffed into his case and the bulk of it would come back creased but unworn.

He was on the road by eight o clock on a sunny Saturday morning and had soon joined the M6 southbound. He hadn't been on a motorway since that fateful day four years ago and he found that he was gripping the steering wheel much harder than usual. He drove at a steady fifty on the inside lane again but when he came to Junction 27 he turned off and took the A49 until he had cleared the stretch where the accident had happened. He just couldn't face driving past the spot. Not yet at any rate. Maybe he never would be able to. He rejoined the motorway again just north of Warrington and continued his way southwards.

His main objective on this trip was to find ways of causing maximum disruption of traffic on the system without endangering human life. It would have to be a concerted campaign of major upset which would cause the greatest delay to freight deliveries. That was the whole point of the exercise. To ensure that major manufacturers became so frustrated with late deliveries that they would seriously consider sending their goods by rail.

If holiday makers, day trippers and business representatives suffered long delays then so be it. Norman hoped that they would be rewarded by clearer roads in the future when most of the monstrous wagons were no longer around.

First of all he must look for suitable locations where there weren't many alternative routes. He needed to find long stretches of motorway away from intersections with other major trunk roads, but as he drove along he realised that he had jumped the gun in this respect. It would have been more efficient had he spent a couple of days studying a large scale map of the motorway network and marking suitable sites. However it was too late to worry about that now he would just have to keep his eyes open.

He had already decided that he would use any method necessary to achieve his objective. Even if it meant resorting to something as extreme as the use of explosives and, deep down, he had the feeling that it would come to that. During his military service he had acquired considerable expertise in the use of small explosive charges used in sabotage and demolition exercises.

Then he started to wonder how he could get hold of supplies of plastic or Semtex explosive, detonators, timers and the like and one name sprang immediately to mind. Ginger Robson. Yes, ex Sergeant Alastair Robson. He could just picture him as he drove along and smiled to himself. That quarter inch crew cut of orangey red hair. The battle scarred face with the permanent grin. Battle scarred, not in any theatre of war, but in the back streets of his native Glasgow. He had left the army several years ago under something of a cloud. Something to do with missing stores and not just the odd tin of corned beef. No Ginger had been siphoning off a variety of explosives, small arms and sundry accessories. Not that anything specific had been proved but the army had made it very clear that if he didn't resign they would prove something and he would spend many long years in the glasshouse. He had decided that it was time to move on any way for he had been screwing the Company Commander's wife and it was only a matter of time before word reached the young officer's ears then the shit would really have hit the fan. He hadn't been too impressed with Robson from the moment he had joined the unit six months earlier.

Yes, Norman decided, he would pay old Ginger a visit.

He was still cruising at a steady fifty miles an hour, keeping a weather eye on the rear view mirror, when he passed under a gantry with signs indicating which lane to take for various destinations. Now that looks promising he thought. It wouldn't take much to drop one of those onto the carriageway. A small charge could be detonated any time during a lull in the traffic. The one thing he was determined must not happen was anything which would endanger human life. Of course, he realised, that would entail being in a position to see the road when the charge was blown. No setting timers and getting as far away as possible. Obviously he would have preferred to be miles away when the explosion took place but if it was necessary to be in view of the target then so be it. He would have to take the risk. It was early days yet and that was only one option.

As he drove further south he noticed that a lot of the overhead gantries that he was passing now were recently constructed and were far more sturdy, being made of reinforced concrete unlike the one which had given him the idea originally. That was quite a flimsy looking affair using a sort of criss-cross metal lattice work forming the uprights and cross members. These new ones, however, were a different proposition all together. It would take quite a large amount of explosive to topple one of these.

Soon he was approaching the Gravely Hill interchange. The notorious "Spaghetti

Junction". As he followed the signs for the M5 he noticed that the gantries had reverted to the older metal type again. But there was a new problem on this stretch. It would be almost impossible to get anywhere near the gantries here without being spotted on one of the many television surveillance cameras which constantly monitored the whole area. Impossible that was unless he was prepared to be completely outrageous. His mind was racing ahead now. An old Ford Transit van painted yellow with the words "Motorway Maintenance" on the sides. A pair of overalls, a hard hat and a few red and white cones. A common enough sight at the roadside these days. Nobody would take the slightest bit of notice he thought. In fact that sort of set up could solve the problem of being in sight of the target and monitoring the traffic flow. Once the explosion happened all attention would be on the ensuing chaos while he could just drive off casually in the van. Yes that had definite possibilities. He was on the M5 now and feeling quite elated. He was also feeling very hungry. Time for a full English breakfast at Frankley Services he thought.

CHAPTER THREE

Norman parked at Frankley Services and climbed the stairs to the cafeteria. He was feeling happier now than he had done for years. He took his tray along the counter and helped himself to a full English breakfast. For the past few years he had rarely eaten anything at all in the morning, normally setting off for work with only a mug of tea inside him. But now, not only were his spirits revived, so was his appetite. He paid for the meal and went looking for a table admiring the view through the large windows at the opposite end of the large eating area. The service area was set on one side of a wide valley and he could see across the rolling fields beyond the motorway to the distant hills. It was a fabulous morning and he felt great. He sat down and sorted everything out on the table and got stuck into the great plateful. As he poured a cup of coffee he noticed her for the first time. She was sat diagonally across the aisle from him and looked like an urban guerrilla. Her dark hair was shaved to within a quarter of an inch of her head. She had gone in for body piercing in a big way, wearing a variety of ornaments in each ear and a small gold ring and a stud in her nose. Norman just how many other parts of her anatomy similarly adorned. She wore a shabby black waistcoat over a rather grubby oversized khaki shirt and a short denim skirt. A very short denim skirt. The most remarkable feature was the length and perfect shape of her well-tanned legs. They were so long and smooth and were only marred by the large black "Doc Martens" into which her feet were thrust. Norman could scarcely keep his eyes off the legs as he ate his breakfast. He was just finishing his last slice of toast and taking yet another furtive glance when she looked in his direction for the first time. Norman felt himself colouring and began to feel suddenly quite warm. She merely grinned and stared back into her empty cup.

Two minutes later she got up from her table, turned and stooped slightly to pick up a huge haversack. The movement emphasised just how short the skirt was and Norman was treated to a momentary flash of pure white undies. He was quite surprised at the effect this had on him. He had felt no sort of sexual urge whatsoever since Jenny had died, but this strange girl had stirred feelings that had been completely dormant throughout the past four years. He realised at that moment he had, unwittingly lived a life of complete celibacy. It had never even occurred to him until now. He had been so immersed in his work. Another thing struck him now when he thought of how he had worked to the exclusion of all else. He was probably quite well off financially. The only money he had spent had been on his modest rent and food for his fairly plain diet. He had also sold the house and after he had repaid the building society he had found to his surprise that he had well over fifteen thousand pounds remaining which he had immediately invested in a high earning savings account.

All this money would come in very handy for his forthcoming campaign. He thought that he might even apply for a six or twelve month leave of absence from work and really throw himself into a concerted offensive of major disruption. He settled back in his chair to enjoy the remains of the coffee pot. Yes it was all falling into place very nicely. He would carry on down the M5 and then onto the M4 and on to London. There must be lots of likely targets on the way, particularly as he got closer to the capital. The volume of traffic around London was absolutely frightening. The M25 alone would probably keep him occupied for months. He drained his cup and went back down the stairs and into the shop where he purchased A to Z maps of Birmingham and London. The motorways immediately surrounding the cities where shown in great detail. He would spend hours studying these maps during the next few weeks. After a quick visit to the toilet he emerged into the sunshine and walked across to where his car was parked.

He filled up the tank at the pumps and pulled out onto the slip road ready to re-join the motorway which looked far busier now. About half way down the slip road he spotted her again. The girl with the legs was standing next to her large back pack holding up a piece of corrugated board with the word "LONDON" scrawled in black marker pen.

Only a week ago he would never have even

considered picking up a hitch hiker let alone one as bizarre looking as this one but, what the hell, he thought, a little bit of company wouldn't come amiss. He could still keep his eyes open while they talked. He pulled over with two wheels on the grass verge and leant over to open the passenger door.

'I can probably take you as far as Slough or maybe Heathrow where I intend staying overnight.'

'That would be absolutely great,' she said and Norman was astounded by the refined accent. He didn't know what sort of accent he had expected, possibly provincial, probably even broad. It just goes to show how very deceptive appearances can be, he thought.

Norman got out and opened the back door and she threw the huge bag in with no effort at all.

'The name's Norman, Norman Parker,' he said as he walked back round to the driver's side and got back into the car.

'Charlie. . . Charlotte Forbes-Smythe,' she replied.

He couldn't get over it. This one was right out of the top drawer by the sound of it, but why the hell was she dressed like some wayward biker. Obviously she was rebelling against something or someone. She eased herself into the seat beside him and stretched her fabulous legs out in front of her very much aware of the effect they were having on Norman Parker. He could be my meal ticket for the next few days if I play my cards right, she thought. He looks as though he could be quite susceptible to a bit of flattery and a night in a hotel close to London sounds very attractive, in fact it would suit me admirably. With that thought in mind she settled back feeling quite contented

'So, Charlie, whereabouts are you headed. Are you going home to visit your parents, or a boyfriend maybe?'

'If you don't ask too many questions Norman Parker and we'll get on just fine. Now tell me something about you.'

'Are you married . . . any children?' She must have sensed that she had said something he found unbearable by the way he gripped the steering wheel until his knuckles were white, or was it the tangible silence. My God you could have cut it with a knife.

'I'm so sorry,' she said with a great amount of concern in her voice, I have obviously touched a very raw nerve.'

'You weren't to know,' his voice was just a hoarse whisper.

'Let's change the subject,' she said quickly, but Norman sensing her acute embarrassment said, 'No, it's OK. It's time I talked about it with someone. I've been bottling it up for far too long,' and he started to tell her the whole painful story. She sat very still and very quiet and as she glanced sideways she saw a tear rolling down his pale cheek. She began to feel terrible about the way she had decided to hit on him for her own selfish ends. She still intended to try and get a night's board and lodging out of him but, now, she thought there is an ideal to repay him. This poor man is desperately in need of some kind of consolation and I am just the girl to provide that.

They were passing the Michael Wood service area when Norman said,

'Right I've told you plenty about me, how about you tell me something about yourself.'

She shrugged her shoulders,

'There's not much to tell really. I have just been thrown out of university. My father recently committed suicide and my mother and brother have completely disowned me.' Norman didn't know whether she was being serious or just taking the piss, but a sideways glance told him that she WAS serious and now it was his turn to feel uncomfortable.

'Do you want to talk about it?' Norman said cautiously.

'I have just discovered, after four years, that pouring it all out to you, a complete stranger, just now has helped enormously. It feels as though a great weight has been lifted. Of course it will never go away completely, but I suddenly feel a little more prepared to move on now.'

'Well it all started two years ago when daddy was made redundant from the Army. He was a Major and had served with his regiment for over nineteen years only to be thrown into the scrap heap due to the need for "cut backs". He was still in his prime at forty two and had seemed all set for further promotion. He was bloody good at his job and the men in his battalion had a great love and respect for him. He was a man's man, a good leader, and a fine sportsman. We had travelled the world with him, my mother, my brother Jeremy and me and never once had we felt in the least bit neglected. He was an excellent husband and father and we all loved him dearly.

The loss of his career however had devastated him. He just wasn't prepared for being suddenly dumped into civilian life. The army had been the only thing he wanted from early on in his school days. He had been in the Cadet Training Scheme at school and had been accepted for the Military Academy at Sandhurst on leaving at the age of sixteen. Then the faceless, heartless bastards in Whitehall had, with the stroke of the pen, completely destroyed his life. Major James Forbes-Smythe became plain Mister. Mummy had been very supportive during those first few months but nothing she could do or say seemed to have any effect whatsoever on his deep depression. Jeremy and I were both away at university so she had to cope more or less on her own. Of course there were the usual counselling sessions which were provided in such circumstances and, although the councillors meant well, they had no success in pulling him out of it. He was a mere shadow of his former self and seemed incapable of finding any sort of motivation.

Anyway, after a few months, mummy tried to

get her own life back to some kind of normality. So, she started playing bridge again each Wednesday afternoon. They had not moved far from the base having bought a lovely detached house on the outskirts of Warminster. It had a beautiful garden and whilst mummy had thought it would keep dad occupied, the bulk of the work had been left to her and a man who came in once a fortnight to do the heavy work. It was after one of her Wednesday afternoons when she returned to find the house empty. She had expected to see daddy slumped in the armchair staring into space as usual but became quite worried as she went about the house calling his name. The house was totally silent. She was almost certain that he would not have gone out anywhere and so she went to look down the garden. She went right down to the orchard at the bottom then turned to go back to the house. Walking back in that direction she could see into the back of the double garage which has doors at each end. To her absolute horror she saw daddy's legs hanging in the wide open doorway and his carpet slippers beneath him on the concrete floor. She half ran, half staggered to the garage and must have fainted when she saw the rictus on dad's face.

She was found half an hour later dazed and confused by a neighbour who had called with some theatre tickets.

The police had called both universities to inform me and my brother of the terrible news. Jeremy returned home the same evening and was a great support to mummy but I lost it completely. I just couldn't handle it. I went on a drunken binge to try and block everything out but it didn't work. Then I resorted to something which revolts me now whenever I think about it. I got hold of some drugs and got into a pretty bad state. I had left my hall of residence at the university and gone to stay with some guys who had dropped out earlier in the year. My family were unable to contact me and the Greater Manchester Police were given the impossible task of trying to track down yet another missing student somewhere on or off the massive campus.

Mummy was absolutely devastated when I didn't turn up for the funeral and, when nine months later, I turned up looking pretty much as you see me now she wouldn't even allow me over the door step. She said that I was a disgrace to my father's memory. My brother was not so reserved and poured abuse on me and said he never wanted anything to do with me again. And so I returned to Manchester and got mixed up with some real low lives. They spouted endless rhetoric mainly about anarchism and the downfall of the system. I was sympathetic to all of this at first because I blamed the establishment for the untimely death of my father. But after a while I began to realise that it was just so much hot air and that I would never achieve anything with those no hopers. So now I am making my way to London to try and make some sort of protest, although short of throwing a bomb through the windows of the Ministry of Defence I am pitifully short of ideas.'

CHAPTER FOUR

Her story had moved Norman and he sat there driving in silence. When she finished she was very quiet also so he decided that it was about time to stop for a coffee. They were just approaching the services at Leigh Delamere. They were on the M4 now and Norman realised that he hadn't even noticed when they had left the M5. So much for keeping his eyes open for likely targets he thought. He pulled off the motorway and up the slip road to the service area.

'Do you fancy a coffee?' Norman asked, glancing sideways,

'You look as though you could do with a break.'

'That would be lovely,' she said leaning back and stretching her arms back behind her head.

They walked into the cafeteria and turned quite a few heads as they did so. Norman realised that they must have looked quite an odd assorted couple but he didn't give a toss. He had changed considerably in the last few hours. He bought two pots of coffee and a couple of Danish Pastries and they made their way to the far end of the room and sat by the window. It was not quite lunch time and the cafe was fairly quiet. They sat down opposite each other and poured their drinks. Norman had, for the first time, noticed just how beautiful she was. You had to look past the silly disguise which she had adopted and there were the classical features. A face full of character with piercing blue eyes and he suspected that her natural hair colour would be blonde, not the jet black which she sported at the moment. Her fingers were long and delicate and, despite the collection of cheap costume rings bearing skulls, swastikas and the like, they were well manicured. Yes, he thought, this is a very classy lady. He felt totally at ease in her company. My God, he thought, I certainly have changed. A week ago I would have run a mile if she had sat at the same table.

'Did you really mean what you said about getting even with those bastards in Whitehall,' Norman ventured very cautiously,

'Because if you are serious I think that we may

be able to do something about that together. You see, I am on a similar mission. I am just starting the planning stage of a campaign of major disruption.'

When she laughed it was one of the most pleasurable sounds he had ever heard. It was music to his ears for he hadn't heard much laughter lately.

'Come on Norman, Your winding me up, I know it.'

Norman was rather taken aback. He had become quite convinced of the feasibility of what he was about to attempt, but deep down he had to admit, that to a complete stranger hearing it for the first time, it must have sounded pretty preposterous.

'No. I'm deadly serious,' and Charlie noting the hurt look on his face replied,

'OK, OK I believe you, but we can't discuss something like this in a public place. If you really are serious we should discuss your plans at length, but somewhere far more private.'

She considered the situation carefully and decided that it was now or never if she was to sleep somewhere in the least bit civilised that night and added, 'Where are you staying tonight? Maybe we could share a room.'

She mentally closed her eyes and waited for the immediate rebuff that she felt sure would come, but was very surprised to hear Norman replying,

'Yes, OK, that sounds like a great idea. I thought I might stay at the Holiday Inn just outside Slough. I have stayed there before and was very comfortable and the food was quite acceptable as I recall.'

Charlie suddenly began to wonder if she'd overplayed her hand and that, maybe it was herself who was being conned. She had never thought it would be so easy. Maybe he was hitting on her, not the other way round. Anyhow, she thought, too late now, I'll just tag along for the time being.

They finished their snack and as they made their way out to the car park the place was beginning to fill up and once again they attracted some curious gazes. Norman in his sober navy blue trousers and pale blue, short sleeved shirt and Charlie looking like a fugitive from some "New Age" commune.

They got back into the car which was now like an oven. The sun was pounding down from a clear blue sky. They wound down the windows and set off as quickly as possible to get some air circulating. They rejoined the motorway and drove along in silence both content just to listen to the radio playing quietly in the background.

It was mid afternoon as they saw the sign announcing that Reading Services were just a mile away. Charlie sat up on seeing the sign and asked,

'Can we pull in here please, I need to go to the ladies.'

'Sure,' replied Norman,

'I wouldn't mind stretching my legs for five minutes.'

He parked the car right opposite the entrance to the ladies toilets and Charlie hopped out and tapped on the back window. When Norman opened the door she dragged out her huge back pack and Norman felt suddenly very dejected. Had he said or done something to upset her he pondered. He felt convinced that she was about to do a disappearing act on him. He should have known it was too good to be true, a lovely girl like that suggesting that they share a hotel room. He walked slowly over to the "take away" counter, bought a can of Coke and took it back to the car, convinced that he would be completing his journey alone. He leant against the bonnet of the car enjoying the ice cold drink and was suddenly aware of someone trying the passenger door. He turned quickly and couldn't believe his eyes.

Charlie was standing there looking completely transformed. Norman stood there with his mouth wide open as she grinned and said,

'Well are you going to open the door or are we going to stand here all afternoon?'

Norman almost tripped over his own feet as he rushed to unlock the door and take the back pack from her. He still couldn't quite take in what he was seeing. Gone were all the body piercing ornaments and the ultra short black hair had been covered up by a very expensive blonde wig. The shoulder length fair hair really suited her. She had exchanged the denim skirt, baggy shirt and waistcoat for a pretty, off the shoulder floral dress which, despite the fact that it must have been stuffed inside the back pack, looked as though it had come straight out of a West End boutique.

'Would you like a coffee or maybe a cold drink,' he managed to stammer.

'That would be lovely,' she smiled, and as they walked towards the cafeteria she added,

'I thought that this might help when we arrive at the hotel. I think that I would have probably been "Persona non Grata" in my other gear.' Norman smiled to himself and thought, yes you're probably right. Once again they turned heads as they entered but for all the right reasons this time. She looked absolutely fantastic and he could see the envious looks in the eyes of most of the men as they walked past, eyes that were saying, 'You lucky bastard, what's a bloke like you doing with someone like that?' and they were probably right. What did she see in him? Norman knew that he was no oil painting. His nickname "Nosey" in the army had not been entirely due to the fact that his surname was Parker. He did have a rather large nose and, as if that weren't enough, his hair was thinning prematurely.

They ate another light snack of sandwiches and coffee, both of them having realised that they hadn't yet had any lunch. Norman had to try very hard to refrain from staring at her as they sat there chatting. He hadn't felt this comfortable with anyone since Jenny and he felt a little twinge of guilt at the thought of her. Not that Jenny would have wanted him to feel like that. She would be the last one to expect that. She would be anxious for him to get on with his life. She would know that he would never forget her.

As they drove towards London the traffic was getting considerably heavier and Norman was glad to turn off at Junction 6 for Slough. They pulled into the car park of the Holiday Inn at about four in the afternoon. As they walked across the foyer towards the reception desk Norman asked nervously whether she would prefer a single room.

'Not unless you particularly want to be alone,' she said quite naturally.

'No, err no, I mean I just thought,' Charlie cut him short, grabbed his arm and said,

'Come along now, don't be so silly, a double will be fine.'

There was absolutely no awkwardness as they signed in under their separate names. The last time Norman had done anything like this had been years ago, long before he and Jenny were married. They had gone down to London for a long weekend and must have had guilt written all over their faces as they had booked in as Mr. and Mrs. Parker. Things were a lot different then. The snooty cow on reception had made them feel about two inches high, and they had spent the entire weekend feeling very uncomfortable.

The room was on the fourth floor but didn't have much of a view. However it was very well appointed and as soon as they had dumped their bags in the corner Charlie had headed straight for the shower. When she emerged ten minutes later wearing only a small hand towel tucked around her, Norman noticed that the lovely smooth tanned skin of her long legs extended to the rest of her body. Long years in the sun while daddy was serving abroad he thought. He just couldn't get over the perfect smoothness of her skin and he longed to stroke her arms, her shoulders, her . . . He snapped himself out of it and looked with exaggerated enthusiasm at the literature which was enclosed with the leather bound menu on the dressing table.

She had noticed him staring and then looking so earnestly at the leaflets. Poor man, she thought, he looks so desperate. He must have been completely unloved since his wife died. He would never let anyone get close to him. He must have been totally racked with guilt. Poor, poor, man. She wanted to go over to him, drop the towel and just hold him close to her body and comfort him but she decided that something as sudden as that would probably scare him off completely. No, she would have to be very careful how she handled him. He was extremely vulnerable at the moment, but she would relieve all that pent up frustration before the night was out. She was determined of that. So instead she said lightly,

'Anything interesting in there? Anything to pass an hour before we go down to dinner?' and she came to sit next to him on the bed. Norman was overcome by the delicate perfume of the shower gel which she had used. Something else from the voluminous back pack. It wasn't the sort of stuff you got in a hotel room. He could feel the damp warmth which her body exuded and it was as much as he could do to keep his hands off her.

We could take a run into Windsor for an hour or so if you fancy, it's just on the other side of the motorway. It's quite pleasant down there by the river.'

Half an hour later they were leaning on the parapet of the bridge leading from Windsor to Eton watching the boats on the river on a very pleasant summer evening.

CHAPTER FIVE

Back in the hotel they went back up to their room to change for dinner. They had spent a very pleasant hour or so just wandering around the old buildings of Eton College and along the bank of the Thames watching the young men practising rowing. Norman could not get over how well they were getting on together. It was all so natural. It was as though they had known each other for ever.

Norman went into the bathroom for a quick shower and a shave. When he came back into the bedroom Charlie was already dressed in a plain pale blue dress of fine clingy material. Once again this dress had miraculously emerged from the large bag completely unscathed. There wasn't a single crease. Norman came to the conclusion that her clothes were of very good quality. She sat in one of the chairs with her beautiful long legs crossed. He couldn't help noticing that she wasn't wearing a bra, the soft material of the dress accentuated the perfect shape of her firm young breasts. Later in the evening he would find that she wasn't wearing anything at all under the dress. It was perhaps as well. He certainly wouldn't have been able to concentrate on the fine meal they were to enjoy that evening.

Norman changed into a pair of dark grey trousers, a crisp white shirt and a plain maroon tie. As they went down in the lift she slipped her arm through his and they came out of the lift like that.

They selected a table for two in an alcove at the far end of the dining room well out of earshot of any of the other diners. When they had given their order to the waiter and chosen a bottle of Leibfraumilch from the extensive wine list they got down to the subject which they had broached earlier in the day at the service area on the M4.

'I can't believe that you were serious when you spoke of causing major disruption,' Charlie said with a slight frown, 'I mean, well, you just don't seem the type. I can imagine you writing letters to the newspapers to get your point across, but I simply can't see you actually getting involved in something illegal.'

'You just can't begin to imagine how angry I have been over the last few years,' Norman replied, 'Every time I see another motorway accident being reported on television it brings all the horror back again. I have come to the conclusion that this carnage will continue so long as we permit those evil monsters to continue rampaging up and down our road system. They are far too big, far too heavy and travel far too fast considering the enormous loads which they haul. They are bloody dangerous and as far as I'm concerned it's high time that all the heavy freight was put back on to the railways where it belongs.'

Charlie noticed a grave change in his mood as he spoke. Although he tried to smile his eyes looked dead. It was as though heavy shutters had fallen behind them.

'What exactly do you have in mind,' she asked reaching across the table and placing a lovely cool hand on top of his.

'I haven't really decided yet,' he said, his real

smile returning,

'But one thing is for certain, I would feel a lot happier with someone like you to share the problem with. Maybe we can help each other to obtain some sort of retribution. You to try and avenge your father's death and me, well you know my reasons. The methods which we use will have to be considered very carefully.' He went suddenly silent as the wine waiter approached and proffered the bottle for his approval.

'Look, I agree in principle to what you are proposing,' she said when the waiter left the table,
'But let's forget it for tonight. Let's just enjoy our meal and each other's company. It seems a shame to spoil the evening with such serious talk.'

Norman nodded his agreement and they settled down to eat and to continue the easy flow of conversation they had enjoyed down by the river. It was almost ten-o-clock by the time they had finished eating and they were sat in two comfortable armchairs in the lounge each cradling a large brandy glass in their hand. Norman could not believe how well they were getting on together. After being cut off from any sort of company, male or female, for the last few years it felt so good.

Half an hour later, after a second brandy, she stood up and held out her hand towards Norman.

'Time to go up I think,' she said softly.

He stood up and took her hand and they made their way over to the bank of lifts in the foyer. On the way up to their floor she put both arms around his neck and kissed him full on the lips. Norman drew back, resisting for a moment. It seemed as though it would be some kind of betrayal if he were to submit, but the thought passed as quickly as it had appeared and he returned her kiss. The bell rang out as the lift reached the fourth floor and they walked out past the couple who were waiting there without even seeing them.

Norman held the door open and Charlie entered the room stepping out of her shoes as she went. She threw her tiny hand bag on to the bed and turned to face Norman as he removed his tie. She looked absolutely gorgeous and he just stood there marvelling at her beauty. Once again she looked at him and thought, poor man, he must be so in need of love that it must be quite painful. She crossed the soft carpet and began to unfasten the buttons of his shirt. He just stood there feeling unsure of himself. It had been so long and he was, once again, feeling slight twinges of guilt. Her long elegant fingers then deftly undid the buckle of his belt and slid down the zip of his trousers. Her hand brushed against his growing erection and she saw him colour slightly.

She stepped slowly back a pace and reached a slim arm up behind her and pulled down the long zip of her little blue dress. With one wonderful swishing sound the dress slid to the floor to reveal her firm naked body. He couldn't help noticing once again that her skin was the same soft even tan colour all over, and he thought again that it must have been the result of many foreign postings with her father. The small thatch of curly fair hair between her legs confirmed what Norman had suspected. She was a natural blonde. The curly hair had been carefully trimmed so that it could be concealed beneath the tiniest bikini, although by the look of the all over tan she had rarely worn anything while she sunbathed. She held out her hand and guided him over to the bed. He clumsily removed his boxer shorts and as she pulled him down on top of her she gently guided him inside her. The soft, wet warmth was too much and he climaxed almost at once. Four years of frustration flooded from him and Charlie just let him flow into her without moving.

'I'm sorry,' he stammered,

'It's been so long since. . .'

'Shush,' she put a finger to his lips,

'It's OK, don't be sorry my love, I know, I know.'

Norman remained hard inside her and began to move far more slowly now and soon Charlie was heaving her hips and enjoying multiple orgasms. They made love for a further half hour and lay back side by side just savouring the moment. Norman could not remember feeling this good for a long time.

The next thing Norman knew, the sun was streaming through partially drawn curtains and he realised that they had both fallen asleep without uttering another word. He looked down at Charlie lying beside him breathing very softly and resisted the urge to caress her lovely body. Instead he slipped into one of the hotel robes and started to make a couple of coffees with the facilities provided. As the cups clinked on their saucers she woke and propped herself up on one arm.

'Morning,' she whispered huskily, 'Sleep well?'

'Like a log,' Norman replied,

'Sorry I fell asleep like that, most ungracious.'

He looked at her longingly as he stood there holding the two cups of coffee.

'Put those down and come here,' she ordered and she spread her arms and legs in an obscene gesture. He was over to the bed like a shot and it was over an hour later as they lay back, exhausted once more. Naturally the coffee was stone cold.

They showered together soaping each other gently and eventually Norman had to force himself to stop. This was not what he had taken time off work for, very pleasant a diversion as it was. No he must get his mind back on track. There was a job to be done.

'We'll just about make breakfast if we hurry,' he said breaking the mood rather abruptly.

'If we must,' she pouted, and ten minutes later

they were on their way down to the dining room.

As Norman dabbed the toast crumbs from the corner of his mouth with the white starched napkin he ventured,

'Well, it's time to get down to some serious planning. You are still with me aren't you. Please say you are.'

'Of course I am, but where do we start?'

'Well I thought that the first thing we should do is to study the maps of the areas surrounding London and Birmingham and look for suitable "targets". Then I thought of visiting an old army mate of mine. He is rather an unsavoury character but he could be a very useful source of "supplies" when we really get started.'

'What sort of supplies?' and for the first time Norman detected a slight note of concern in her voice.

'You are surely not considering explosives and guns and things are you?'

'I thought that you were serious about all of this,' he said with a slight edge to his voice.

'Of course I am,' she said rather hesitantly,

'Of course I'm serious, it's just that you surprise me, even scare me a little sometimes.'

'Look,' said Norman quietly, 'If you want out I would quite understand. I admit it could all get a bit heavy. Its better you get out now, the less you know about my plans the better, for both our sakes.'

'No, damn you Norman Parker. What are you saying? That I'm scared or that I have no commitment.'

She had spoken rather more loudly than she had intended and several heads turned in their direction. The heads quickly turned away again, the assumption being that it was just a lovers tiff.

'Fine then, if you're sure I think we should make a move and find some slightly cheaper accommodation. Perhaps somewhere in South London. The last I heard of old "Ginger" he was frequenting a pub down Wandsworth way. We'll carry on into London on the M4, get on to the South Circular and look for a cheap bed and breakfast place somewhere in the Richmond or Putney area.'

They went back up to pack their few belongings, settled the account and were on the road by nine thirty. Being Sunday there was no rush hour traffic to slow them down and they made good progress towards the city. It was another fine sunny day and Norman felt quite pleased with himself. He was actually starting to do something practical and the best thing was that he now had a partner in crime. As they left the motorway onto the A307 and followed the signs for Kew and Richmond they were both singing along happily to a "sixties" song on the radio. Funny, Norman thought, how everybody, young or old, always seemed to know the words of "sixties" songs.

CHAPTER SIX

They found a nice little private hotel on Upper Richmond Road close to East Putney tube station. They booked a room for a week initially and paid in advance. The deal included dinner, bed and breakfast and was quite reasonably priced for accommodation in the capital.

It was a very clean, comfortable establishment run by a jolly Irish widow, Mrs. O'Donnel. She was a small, rotund lady with a ruddy complexion and a permanent smile. The two things she enjoyed in life seemed to be cleaning and cooking, an ideal combination for her chosen career. She made Charlie and Norman feel completely at home and adopted an almost motherly interest in them.

They settled into their room and took one of the A to Z's each and started to study them, making frequent circles on likely sites with black felt tip markers. These were only initial suggestions and they would have to actually drive around the motorways to inspect them. They worked away in silence as they had agreed. They would then have an in depth discussion to see if they both agreed on the preliminary list later. This was going to be very much a joint effort. In the middle of the afternoon there was a tap on the door. It was Mrs. O'Donnel with a tray containing a large pot of tea and two large slabs of fruit cake. She said that she hoped that she wasn't interrupting and bustled out of the room asking them to bring the tray back with them when they came down to dinner.

They stopped what they were doing and devoured the cake and enjoyed two good strong cups of tea apiece. Once again they had been so absorbed in what they were doing that had missed out on lunch. While they were having their tea break Norman suggested that they should make a start on trawling around the local pubs after dinner that evening. They decided to start working out from the hotel towards Wandsworth town centre. Ginger had been a bit vague when he had last phoned Norman about six months ago. Norman had a sneaking suspicion that he was being deliberately evasive about his whereabouts, no doubt as a result of some shady dealing or other. He hadn't mentioned anything about a flat or house, just that he was doing a lot of business in a pub down Wandsworth way. When Norman had pressed him to be more precise Ginger had waffled and said that all he needed to do was mention his name and someone would point him in the right direction. The more he thought about it the more he doubted whether he should involve Charlie with his ex army mate, but when he broached the subject she almost exploded and said,

'Look, we are either in this together, and I mean in everything together, or I think that we should forget the whole thing!'

'OK, OK, sorry I spoke,' said Norman holding up both hands in mock defence.

'Just so long as we understand each other,' she said punching him playfully on the shoulder,

'And another thing has just struck me,' she continued,

'I think that I will revert to my alter ego for

our trips around the local hostelries. I think that I would feel a tiny bit vulnerable in a flimsy dress and high heels. One thing I've noticed when I am wearing my other gear is that I get almost no hassle at all from men. I don't think they know how to take me, anyway it works a treat. I think it might be an idea if you were to dress down a bit. Blend into the background so to speak. No point sticking out like a sore thumb on an errand like this .'

Norman was beginning to realise that she was going to be more of an asset than he had thought. Her years in the wilderness had certainly made her far more street wise than he was.

It was about four in the afternoon when Charlie suggested that they avail themselves of the shower before the other guests started using all the hot water. She threw a towel over her shoulder and headed down the passage. Ten minutes later she was back with the large bath towel wrapped around her. One thing about her closely cropped hair, it didn't take much washing and drying. Norman took his shower and came back acknowledging the wisdom of using the facilities when they had. The water was already running tepid as he had finished. That was something they would have to remember for the rest of their stay.

Charlie was lying on her towel looking extremely inviting when he got back into the room. She beckoned him over and they just lay there caressing each other gently. Charlie had decided that it was far too hot for anything else just now but had hinted that all that may change later on when it was a bit cooler. Norman felt like going back and taking another shower. A cold one this time.

After a very filling three course meal they walked out of the small Kilkenny Hotel at about half past eight. They walked hand in hand down Upper Richmond Road which, even at that time on a Sunday evening, was quite busy being part of the South Circular gyratory system. The first pub they came to was the Northumberland Arms. They walked into the saloon bar and attracted hardly a glance as they made their way to the bar.

'What do you fancy,' said Norman who was surveying the vast array of pumps along the highly polished mahogany bar top.

'I think we had better stay on halves if we are

embarking on a pub crawl,' she replied,

'I'll have a half of Carlsberg please.'

Norman finally attracted the attention of a large busted barmaid in her late forties,

'Two halves of Carlsberg please,' he said proffering a five pound note. Two tall slim glasses were placed on the bar and the condensation was already forming against the pale amber background as Norman picked up his change from a pool of lager. He handed one to Charlie and took a long draught from his own glass. The first half was gone in a couple of minutes, it was an extremely hot and humid evening. Clasping their second halves, they jostled their way through the crowd and placed them on a small circular shelf which ran around one of the supporting columns in the middle of the room. They stood there surveying the crowd in the bar. They were certainly a mixed bunch, male and female, old and young and as Norman turned a full circle he noticed an older man standing alone round the other side of the column.

'I wonder if you can help me,' he started.

'You'll have to speak up son, I'm a bit Mut and Jeff.'

Norman started again speaking louder this time,

'I'm looking for a bloke called Robson, Ginger Robson, ex army type.'

'Sorry mate, can't say I know him. Try asking Rita over there,' he was pointing at the barmaid who had served them earlier, She knows everybody round here. Right nosey cow she is. Wants to know everything about everybody that one.'

'Thanks,' said Norman and he started to guide Charlie back to the bar. He headed up to the far end were Rita was serving five or six youngsters who didn't really look old enough to be out this late let alone being served in a pub. He beckoned her over when she had finished serving the lads and asked her if she knew Ginger Robson.

'Sorry dear,' she shook her head, her large ear rings swinging violently from side to side,

'Can't say as I've heard of a Ginger Robson, and I know most of the blokes as comes in here,' she gave Norman a knowing wink and, turning towards an older man who was probably the landlord, she shouted along the bar,

'You know anybody called Ginger Robson,

Sid?'

'Never heard of 'im,' Sid's voice was low and gravelly and sounded for all the world like his namesake Sid' James of "Carry on" fame.

Norman and Charlie, having said 'thanks anyway,' drained their glasses and headed for the door. They had made a preliminary list from the yellow pages which included several pubs in the Putney area. The Maltese Cat, The Castle on Putney Bridge Road, The Green Man on Putney Heath, The Highwayman and several others. Norman realised as soon as they had left the pub that they should have asked directions to their next port of call and he was just turning back to enquire when a tall thin black boy with ridiculous blonde curly hair and dressed in a floor length leather coat which flapped open to reveal a white suit, stopped him in his tracks. Norman's first reaction was that he was about to be mugged and backed off. The black boy raised a yellowish white palm and said,

'Yoah, cool it man. You was asking about a dude called Robson back there yeah? Well I think I might be able to help if you make it worth my while.' Norman turned to Charlie who nodded.

'OK!' he said 'Tell me what you know and we'll see what it's worth.'

'I know where that robbing red headed honkey bastard is hanging out dese days. One of the "brothers" runs a few Toms in Praed Street, just behind Paddington Station. Say he saw Robson in a pub called The British Standard. I'ts on a corner somewhere between Praed Street and Sussex Gardens. You tell him if you find him that Winston B' says to watch his back if he ever come round dis turf again.'

Norman nodded his thanks and pressed a fiver into the large pale palm. The black lad muttered something quite uncomplimentary and shuffled back towards the Northumberland.

'Well that should save us quite a bit of leg work, Charlie, but it's a bit late to start trailing over the river now. We'll try tomorrow evening. Why don't we go back now that it has cooled down.'

'I don't think that you've cooled down any, quite the opposite, but I'm not complaining. Come on let's get to it. I just hope that ancient bed doesn't make too much racket. We don't want Mrs. O'Donnel getting the wrong idea. She might cut off our tea and cakes in the afternoons and that would be a shame,' and with that she linked arms with him and they made their way back looking forward to another wonderful night. Norman mused as they strolled back to the "Kilkenny" that this lady was the best thing that had happened to him in a long time. He was beginning to slowly lose the feelings of guilt which he had felt when he had first made love to Charlie. He was starting to convince himself that Jenny would be the last one to expect him to remain celibate for the rest of his life. He clasped Charlie's hand tighter and she seemed to sense what he was thinking and just tightened her grip with his.

CHAPTER SEVEN

The following morning it was still very hot and sunny and, after another of Mrs. O'Donnel's enormous breakfasts, Norman suggested that, instead of sitting in their room checking the maps, they could take them to a park somewhere and continue the job out in the fresh air. They walked down to the tube station, boarded the first District Line train for Upminster and got off at St. James's Park.

It was very pleasant sitting on one of the park benches alongside the lake and after about an hour of marking their respective A to Z's, Norman strolled over to the ice cream van and bought two large "99" cornets. They sat there enjoying the sunshine like a couple of tourists. At lunchtime they walked up the Mall, through

Admiralty Arch and passing The National Gallery on their right they made their way up Whitcomb Street and had their lunch at the Kentucky Fried Chicken place in Coventry Street. Charlie was quite surprised at Norman's knowledge of London's West End,

'Not bad for a Northerner,' she said sarcastically and he explained that he had spent a lot of time working down there on exhibitions and had spent most of his spare time exploring the city on foot. The only way to see the place in his opinion.

After lunch as they were walking round Piccadilly Circus Norman had suggested that, in order to save time that evening, they could hop on a tube train up to Edgeware Road and look for the "British Standard" during the afternoon. They could do it on one train from here on the Bakerloo Line. He was just showing off now and Charlie smiled to herself. They took the ancient cage like lift up to street level at Edgeware Road and emerged, blinking, into the bright sunlight. They walked down to the corner of Sussex Gardens to the pelican crossing to stand any chance at all of crossing the busy road. The pub, as it turned out, didn't take much finding. They discovered it after about ten minutes on the corner of Bouverie Place and Star Street, just as the man had said, between Praed Street and Sussex Gardens.

They walked back to Edgeware road tube station and got the train back down to East Putney. Back in the hotel they both showered in reasonably hot water and dressed ready for the evening. Despite what she had said the previous evening about her clothing she put on a white pleated mini skirt and a pale peachy coloured crop top.

'Well,' she said as Norman raised an eyebrow, Norman wasn't complaining. She looked absolutely stunning and as they went down to the dining room, Mrs. O'Donnel did a double take. She must have thought that Norman had two girls up in his room.

Later in the evening they were sat in a corner of the "British Standard", each with a half of lager, keeping an eye on the door. Charlie had been right to wear the clothes she'd chosen earlier. It was really quite a pleasant little place and a lot of the customers were middle aged couples. It was getting on for half past ten and they were beginning to think that they'd had a wasted journey when the door opened and there he was. Norman was shocked by his appearance. Gone was the smart military bearing of Colour Sergeant Robson. This man looked a wreck by comparison. He was dressed in scruffy khaki drill trousers and an ill fitting camouflage jacket. The only thing that hadn't changed was the bright red crew cut hair. Had it not been for the hair and the fact that they had expected to see him there, Norman would never have recognised him. They let him order his drink before going over to join him at the bar.

'All right, Ginger, mate,' and Norman was shocked as he spun round with a haunted look on his face.

'Bloody hell,' he said, sounding quite relieved,

'Nosey Parker, what the fuck are you doing here. Och, sorry hen, excuse the French.'

'Don't bother about me,' she said still smirking at the nickname. "Nosey" she thought, I should have known there would have to be a nickname having spent most of my life around army bases.

Norman was quite concerned about his old friend. He looked as though he had been sleeping rough, or at best, not looking after himself as he should.

'You're looking a bit rough Ginger old mate.'

'Oh cheers, make a bloke feel great why don't you?'

' Look you two, why don't we take a pew,' said Charlie pointing back towards the corner.

'You look as though you have a bit of catching up to do.'

As they sat down Ginger looked enquiringly towards Charlie.

'Oh I'm sorry mate,' said Norman,

'This is Charlie, well Charlotte actually. She's helping me with a little project at the moment. That's why I've come to look you up. I am hoping that you can help me as well.'

'I don't know about that at the moment Norman. I'm having a few problems just now. About six months ago I got mixed up with some pretty heavy company. I was approached by this strange black kid one night in a pub. Apparently he'd heard I was doing a bit of dealing in small arms and explosives. Said he was a runner for one of the big South London outfits. I should have seen the writing on the wall straight away. Those guys don't play softball. Anyway I obtained a few items for them and the money was far better than I'd been making from the small time punks I'd been dealing with. They had obviously been trying me out for, two or three weeks later, the same runner tracked me down and placed a very large order. He handed me a package containing £2,000 saying that it was just a retainer and that they needed the goods pretty bloody quickly. I would receive the balance on delivery. The shopping list he gave me frightened the shit out of me. I was well out of my depth. When the delivery date arrived I hadn't managed to get a fraction of the order and so I had to front up, hand back the retainer and admit defeat. They weren't at all pleased and told me that if I knew what was good for me I should get off their patch and not return. As most of my clientele operated in the area it was a disaster. Overnight my thriving little business had gone down the tubes. I heard a few weeks later that a big blag down Catford way had been cancelled and that there were some very unhappy villains down there.'

'So what the hell have you been doing for the last few months?' asked Norman the concern showing on his face.

'Well I got this really crappy room at the back of Paddington. It's a real rat hole but it's all I can afford until I build up a few contacts in the area. It's a painfully slow job. I imagine the word's been put around.'

'This runner you spoke of, wasn't a black kid with blonde hair by any chance? Name of Winston B'?

'Jesus Christ,' gasped Ginger, looking absolutely staggered.

'How the hell did you know that? My God, they're not using you to get at me are they?'

'No, relax. I think they already know where you can be found. It was Winston who told me where you were hanging out these days. He just happened to be in the Northumberland Arms when I was making enquiries about you and he asked me to pass on a message if I found you. Calm down mate, you're a bag of nerves. Oh, and by the way, the message was to keep away from your old haunts in South London.'

'Surprise, Sur-bloody. . .prise.'

'Well the first thing we must do is to get you some decent accommodation", said Norman, I've got a bob or two stashed away. It's the least I can do considering the way you looked after me down in the Falklands.'

Charlie nodded in approval and Norman went on, 'There are lots of good bed and breakfast places just around the corner in Sussex Gardens. It's a pity we can't take you back to Mrs. O'Donnel's. Now that is a good place, but in the present circumstances I don't think that would be a very good idea do you?'

Saying that they finished their drinks and told Ginger to go and collect his belongings and to meet them back at the pub. Norman didn't think it was a good idea for Charlie, looking as gorgeous as she did, to go anywhere near Ginger's seedy residence.

Ginger was back within quarter of an hour with a large ex-army holdall containing all his worldly goods, well all his legal possessions that is. They made their way to a very decent looking private hotel on Sussex Gardens and paid the landlady, who was looking at Ginger with a doubtful expression on her face, for a week in advance.

Norman joked, 'Don't worry love, he scrubs up quite well,' and turning to his old army pal he added,

'You won't give the lady any trouble will

you?'

The unsmiling landlady still looked very doubtful.

They left a happier looking Ginger waving on the doorstep and made their way back towards Edgeware Road tube station having arranged to see him at ten-o-clock the following morning. It was still quite warm and humid despite the fact that it was now going up for midnight.

CHAPTER EIGHT

They reluctantly decided, whilst sitting in the tube back to East Putney, that there wasn't much point in staying at Mrs. O'Donnel's now. They may just as well move in with Ginger for a few days. They informed her of their decision to go and stay with their friend at breakfast the following morning and Norman had insisted that she kept the advance money which he had paid her, insisting that she should not, under any circumstances, be out of pocket because of their change of plans.

Norman packed their luggage into the car and carefully backed it out of one of the two precious parking spaces at the rear of the building. He had been more than happy to leave the car there for the duration of their stay saying that a car was far more trouble than it was worth in London these days.

They were fortunate enough to find another parking space in one of the inner roads which are separated from the main road by gardens which give the Sussex Gardens its name. It was about a hundred yards from Ginger's hotel and having booked themselves in provisionally for two days they went upstairs and knocked on Ginger's door.

The person who opened the door was much more like the old Sergeant Robson Norman had known. He had obviously showered, was clean shaven and was dressed in navy blue chinos and a white T shirt.

'Come in the both of ye,' his voice much lighter than the previous evening.

'Have a seat. Now what's this project you were on about last night? I believe you said the wee lassie here is helping you.'

'NO!' Charlie rebuked him,

'The wee lassie is a fully committed partner in the project!'

'Oh dear,' said Ginger raising his hands in mock horror,

'Have I put my big size nines in it? I'm sorry. What is this project you're both working on then?'

Norman told him the whole story starting with the accident and continuing with how he had met Charlie and how they had decided on a mutual course of action. When he had finished Ginger was looking very serious and said,

'Jesus, Norman. As our American cousins would say. . . this is pretty heavy shit man! Are you serious the pair of you?'

'Deadly serious, and that's where you come in. We'd like you to be our Quartermaster supplying us with those items in which you specialise. What do you think? Are you with us?'

'Nosey, old mate, if you have got the money and if you are really serious then I'm your man. Have you made up a shopping list yet?'

'Well no, we were hoping to be guided by you. Any suggestions would be most welcome.'

'Let me have half a day or so to do some calculations. You two go off and enjoy yourselves and we'll talk again after dinner tonight, OK.'

Ginger spent the rest of the morning working out what they would need in the way of plastic explosive, detonators and remote control gear. He based his calculations partly on what

Norman had told him but mainly on many years of experience in the business. In the afternoon he went to the lock-up where he had quickly hidden his stock following his hasty departure from south of the river. By four o clock he had made up a sample radio controlled explosive device ready to show to the two "would be" saboteurs later that evening.

In the meantime Charlie and Norman had spent a very pleasant day behaving like a couple of tourists, strolling about hand in hand. They had taken the Docklands Light Railway from Tower Hill out to Island Gardens and had walked through the foot tunnel to Greenwich. Sitting outside the Trafalgar Tavern, not far from the "Cutty Sark", they had enjoyed a pie and a pint. Then after sitting on a bench facing the river for an hour or so they boarded a pleasure boat back to Westminster Pier.

Just after six they returned to their new hotel to be greeted by a curt,

'Dinner's at seven,' by the surly landlady. How different from Mrs. O'Donnel thought Norman as they climbed the stairs to their room. They both flopped on the bed, pleasantly tired after their day of sightseeing. As they got dressed for dinner, Norman noted that, on the odd occasions when Charlie actually wore undies, she wore very pretty undies. The sort that he had often admired in the mail order catalogues. Jenny had been very practical in that department, always sticking to good old Marks and Sparks plain cotton. Charlie was standing in front of the dressing table mirror wearing a pale blue lacy bra and matching panties. The sort with lots of delicate lace and a waistline which dipped in a "V" to reveal a very neat navel. She noticed his admiring looks through the mirror and said with a chuckle,

'Down boy. We'll be late for dinner, and we don't want to upset Mrs. Whatsit do we?'

'Sod Mrs. Whatsit' thought Norman, but he continued to get dressed and ten minutes later they were on their way down to the dining room in the basement.

The food, in fairness, was very good and after a very enjoyable meal they adjourned to Ginger's room. They settled down, Charlie on the only chair in the room and Norman on the bed while Ginger produced three cans of lager from the bottom of the wardrobe. After a quick swig from his can he then returned to the wardrobe and produced a small cardboard box.

Inside the box was a small black rectangular plastic case with a thick wad of Plasticine on the back.

'This will stick to almost anything allowing the device to be placed quite accurately so that it causes the maximum damage.'

Ginger slid back the top of the box to reveal what looked like more Plasticine but which was actually plastic explosive. Alongside this was a tiny radio receiver which was connected by means of a fine red wire to a detonator which was embedded in the explosive. From another cardboard box he produce a very compact radio transmitter which, he told them, had a range of about a quarter of a mile. However, he added, two hundred to two hundred and fifty yards would be an ideal distance. Norman was thinking to himself that that would present no problem if they were to use the "Motorway Maintenance" van idea.

'That tiny thing will topple a motorway gantry?' asked Charlie looking very doubtful.

'Nay problem lassie,' Ginger assured her,

'Tomorrow morning we will go somewhere deserted and have a little demonstration and I'll show you just what this little beauty can do.'

They all piled into Norman's car the following morning with Ginger in the driving seat. He drove across London using roads which Norman had never even heard of, despite his reasonably good knowledge of the capital and soon they were crossing Tower Bridge. Once over the bridge they turned left into Tooley Street heading east along the A200. They carried on until they joined the A206 through Woolwich. At Thamesmead West they took the A2106 Western Way passing Belmarsh Prison on their right. Over to the left of them lay a vast open area facing the London City Airport on the opposite bank of the Thames. Ginger turned off the road on to a rough cinder track and headed for the river. He pulled up beside a rusting power pylon which looked as though it hadn't been used for years. There were no cables attached to the insulators hanging limply from its arms. They got out of the car and Norman's nostrils were assailed by the strange mixture of smells of a river as it approaches its estuary. Mud, salty air and rotting vegetation and it felt quite cool out in this desolate place after the heat of the city centre.

'Right,' said Ginger, 'I would imagine that this pylon here is much bigger than anything you have envisaged tackling on the motorways,' and saying that he walked around the base of the structure and finally bent down to place the little black plastic box about eighteen inches up on one of its legs.

He told them to get back into the car, drove on towards the river for about three hundred yards and stopped again. He got out of the car and produced a small pair of high powered binoculars. He scanned the surrounding area quite slowly and suddenly lowered the glasses and blinked his eyes to rid them of the dazzle he had experienced from the sun bouncing off the pyramid shaped roof of the Canary Wharf Tower in the distance towards the city. He waited for a few minutes until the kaleidoscope of brilliant colours had cleared from his vision and then he began to slowly scan a full three hundred and sixty degrees again. Satisfied that the area was clear of prying eyes he got back into the car and wound down the window. They were parked sideways on to the pylon and taking out the tiny transmitter he pointed it at the large rusty structure.

They saw the small flash a second or so before they heard the muffled boom and experienced the slight pressure shock, mainly in their eardrums. Nothing seemed to happen at first and then, as in a slow motion film, the pylon began to topple then fall quite quickly to disappear in a cloud of dust. This was immediately followed by a second explosion. A great flock of sea gulls burst out of some dead ground between themselves and the river. They rose spiralling into the air screeching their noisy protest at the rude interruption of their scavenging on some rotting rubbish in the hollow. Ginger was out of the car again with the glasses and within seconds he was back in the car and was driving back to the road satisfied that his little demonstration had gone unnoticed.

In reality it hadn't gone unnoticed. About half a mile away in a small brick shed with only half of its asbestos roof remaining, Shamus Hennesey mumbled incoherently,

'Jeysus, did you see that Morphy? The bloody thing just disappeared so it did.'

He lifted the bottle, still sheathed in its brown paper bag, and took a long drink of the cheap red plonk

There was, sadly, no Murphy there to hear him. Poor old Murphy had died of hyperthermia two years before but Shamus, in his permanently inebriated state, still spoke to him as though they were still together, so this particular observation would never be relayed to anyone else. And even if it ever was, it wouldn't be taken very seriously.

Ginger turned the car back towards the city and as they drove along he asked,

'Well lassie does that answer your question of last evening? I think that was pretty convincing, don't you.'

Charlie had to admit that she was certainly impressed and Norman nodded in silent agreement. These small devices would suit his requirements admirably. But then he had never doubted that Ginger would come up with the goods.

CHAPTER NINE

Back at the hotel Norman asked Ginger how soon he could put together ten or twelve of the devices.

'It shouldn't take more than a couple of days. When do you propose starting your campaign?'

'Within the week,' replied Norman,

'No point hanging about. We will spend the next few days driving around checking the locations which we have already marked on the maps. There is one other thing that you might be able to help us with however.'

'What's that then?' asked Ginger.

'What are the chances of getting your hands on a decent Ford Transit. Three or four years old, preferably yellow and in good condition. We don't want traffic cops picking us up for having a dodgy looking vehicle. Whilst we are driving around I intend looking for Motorway Maintenance vans and taking down genuine registration numbers. I will want at least three sets of plates making up which can be traced through Swansea and found to be exactly what the van purports to be.' I would also like three sets of sign written plates saying "Motorway Maintenance" which can be very quickly bolted on and more importantlyquickly removed.

'That shouldn't be too difficult. I have quite a few mates in the motor trade. The shady end of the trade that is. Leave it with me. With a bit of luck I should have one stashed in the lock up by the end of the week. That gives you three days to do your driving around.'

Charlie and Norman checked out, said their goodbyes to Ginger and set off North up the A5 Edgeware Road. Up through Kilburn, Cricklewood and on up to the M1 at Staples Corner. They were soon passing Scratchwood Services and Norman turned to Charlie,

'Look I've been thinking. When we have finished looking around the Birmingham area, concentrating on the M6, M5 interchange we really ought to look for a base for our operations. We don't want to be chasing up and down the motorways unnecessarily. Not only would it be non productive and expensive fuel wise, it would draw unwanted attention to us and the vehicle. We can do without that. I thought that if we are going to concentrate on the areas around the Midlands and London we need to be somewhere in the triangle formed by the M5, M4 and M40. Possibly somewhere in the Cotswolds. Burford, or Cirencester for instance. Equidistant from the M4 at Swindon and the M5 at Gloucester with fast and easy access to both. What do you think?'

'That's a great idea Norman, but let's get one job done at a time eh!. Let's get this recce' done first and then get back down to London and see how Ginger is getting on with our supplies and transport.'

Norman nodded, 'You're quite right of course. Method and meticulous planning, that's the secret.'

The traffic was surprisingly light on the motorway and they were making excellent progress. As they drove through the pleasant Home Counties countryside passing Bushey to their left Charlie noticed a yellow van a few cars ahead on the inside lane. It was a motorway maintenance van and as Norman fell in behind it she took down its registration number. They followed it until it took the slip road at Junction 6A, the turn off for the M25.

'That's our first set of registration plates taken care of,' said Charlie and, having further suggested that they stop for lunch at Watford Gap, she settled down in the passenger seat and immediately nodded off.

They were running parallel to the West Coast main railway line doing just over seventy and being easily overtaken by the Intercity train which was also travelling north as Norman gently shook her awake.

'Almost time for our lunch stop,' and just as he had said it they passed the sign reading services one mile. After a light lunch they set off again and were soon turning onto the M6. The traffic was heavier now as they approached the Birmingham conurbation and this was no bad thing. They needed to be travelling relatively slowly in order to make their observations.

They were well past the Coventry turn off's when they spotted another maintenance van. Charlie noted the index number as it took the

M42 exit to Solihull. Set number two taken care of Norman thought and this one would probably be registered to one of the Midlands County Councils. Between junctions seven and eight, as they were approaching M5 turn off the traffic was almost at walking pace. They turned onto the M5 and one of the first things that struck Norman was the fact that the first closed circuit television camera they passed was facing away from them monitoring traffic coming in the opposite direction. In other words they could approach it without being spotted. That was a possibility he hadn't considered. Toppling a camera mast would produce double the chaos he thought and mentioned the same to Charlie who agreed enthusiastically.

They were travelling along the elevated section now passing West Bromwich to their left. They spotted two more camera masts, one of which was also facing in the opposite direction. Ideal they both agreed. It was going better than they had anticipated. The camera masts would be far easier targets than the overhead gantries and would be far less likely to cause human casualties. Of course what they had not considered, and what they would only realise months later when the IRA started their campaign of transport disruption, was that, all that was required was a telephone threat which would prompt the police to clear the motorways for miles around. Of course in order for that to work one required the necessary code which the terrorist organisations normally changed from time to time.

Feeling quite satisfied with themselves, they turned off the motorway at junction five for Droitwich and booked into a Motor Lodge for the night. Having had a meal at the adjoining "Little Chef" they turned in for an early night, although not necessarily for an early sleep.

The following morning they set off down the motorway towards the M4 and London. They had decided to concentrate on the Midlands first and then move on to the London area later depending how successful their first attempts had been. They were heading back now to see how Ginger was getting on. They were driving on a comparatively clear road and singing along to the radio. Norman still couldn't get over just how well they got on together. It was so good that he occasionally felt a stab of guilt when he thought of Jenny.

They arrived back at Sussex Gardens shortly after two in the afternoon and were greeted once again by the surly landlady who told them that Ginger was not in and that she had no idea when he would be back. Still her charming old self thought Norman and asked with a big smile on his face,

'Any chance of a double room for a couple of days?'

She agreed with a disgusted look on her face which indicated to Norman that the money for the room had only just taken precedence over her disapproval of him and Charlie sharing a room under her roof. And so, just to annoy her they made love very noisily during the afternoon. About five o clock there was a sharp knock on the door and they were almost hoping that it was Mrs. Whatsit coming to complain about the noise but it was Ginger.

Whether it was the state of the bed or the silly grins on their faces, Norman didn't know but Ginger gave him a knowing wink and asked,

'Had a busy afternoon planning strategy, ugh? Just as well some of us really have been busy,' and with that he threw a large cardboard box on the bed.

'One dozen items as requested. The van will be ready Saturday morning. I've decided to add a few refinements which should make life a bit easier for you both when you become active.'

After another excellent dinner, ('You can say what the hell you want about Mrs. Whatsit but she's a bloody rare cook,' observed Ginger,) they went over to the "British Standard" for a few beers. They arrived back at the digs just before eleven, all three of them slightly the worse for wear.

As they staggered up the wide stone steps to the front door Ginger sniggered as Norman tripped,

'That'll put a stop to your fun and games for tonight you randy bastard.'

'You're only jealous,' said Charlie who was slurring her words.

'Bloody right I am lassie,' and he laughed ironically as he himself tripped over the top step.

'Seriously though, I think that you're the best thing that has happened to Norman in a long time. Good luck to the both of yous,' and with that he gave Charlie an avuncular kiss on the forehead and bade them both good night.

CHAPTER TEN

Ginger hadn't been joking when had told them about the few "extras" on the van. They all went down to the lockup on Saturday morning and he listed the refinements with pride.

'The engine has been tuned by an expert,' Ginger told them. 'Billy Ingham was the best "wheels man" in the business. He was never ever caught during a long and distinguished career of crime. I had him do up the engine just in case you ever need to make a hasty departure from any particular situation.'

Norman stood there with a worried look on his face,

'I never envisaged a situation where we may have to make a quick getaway, but of course, you are quite right. It always pays to be prepared for any contingency.'

Ginger continued to show them the other "extras" on the van. The two side panels had been ingeniously converted so that they flipped over on central spigots. In one position the sides of the van read,

"Motorway Maintenance",

then whilst Charlie and Norman stood alongside, Ginger slipped inside and the panels smoothly rotated to reveal two green panels which announced in gold sign writing of a very high quality,

J. Simpson & Son, Landscape Gardeners.

It really was very impressive. The operation could be carried out quite quickly without any need to leave the vehicle. The two rear windows had been re-glazed with one way glass, enabling the occupants to watch a potential target without being observed from the outside.

'And now for the *Piece de Resistance*,' said Ginger with a flourish. He pulled up two concealed ring handles from the floor and raised the two halves of the floor up to the sides of the van. The joint down the centre of the floor had been made with the precision and skill of a time served cabinet maker. The wood had been suitably stained to indicate long and hard use as a working vehicle and Norman had never noticed the hairline joint. Below the false floor lay a double mattress and on seeing that Charlie coloured slightly and spoke for the first time.

'What the hell's that in aid of Sergeant?' she said in her most upper crust voice.

' My God,' said Ginger, 'You sound just like the C.O.'s wife. Don't get upset lassie, the mattress has a perfectly practical purpose. It is there in case you have to lie low for any reason. Might as well be comfortable. You may have to spend quite a long time in hiding or merely observing a situation.'

She caught Norman smirking out of the corner of her eye, 'Just so long as you don't get any cute ideas. This is purely for business, O.K.'

'You will find two compartments behind the drivers and passengers seats,' Ginger continued. 'These contain emergency rations and drinking water. One of them also contains the explosive devices and two very special items which I sincerely hope you will never need.'

Norman felt the hairs on the back on his neck standing erect.

'What sort of special items are we talking about?'

He didn't really need to ask and the knowledge abruptly focused his mind on the seriousness of the mission on which they were about to embark.

'They are there only for use in the most desperate of situations, and as I have said, the chances are that you will never even have to remove them from their well concealed hiding place. Oh, and speaking of desperate situations, calls of nature can be answered by means of a very basic hole in the floor beneath the mattress.'

Charlie grimaced, 'Oh my God, that is really charming I must say.'

'If ye canny take a joke lassie, ye shouldne hay joined,' chuckled Ginger, reverting to his most basic Glaswegian.

On a rack suspended from the roof at the back of the seats was a selection of hard hats, day-glow jackets and red and white road cones together with a couple of powerful torches and some battery operated flashing orange lights. Ginger, it seemed, had thought of everything.

Back at Sussex Gardens Norman sat in the van

and Charlie was at the wheel of his car directly behind as they said their goodbyes to Ginger.

'Thanks a lot mate,' said Norman with genuine gratitude,

'I knew that you would come up with the goods. So many things I would never have thought of, a real professional job. Thanks again, and remember, if you need anything at all, I mean anything, to help you get back on your feet, you only have to ask. You have my mobile number.''

With that he pulled away from the kerb side and as he looked in the wing mirror he saw Ginger stick his head through the car window and give Charlie a kiss on the cheek as she pulled out and followed him.

Norman felt the adrenaline pumping as they drove through Hammersmith heading for the Great West Road which would take them onto the M4 motorway.

They were soon approaching Heston Services where they had arranged to meet up should they get separated in the traffic of West London. They arrived within minutes of each other and as they sipped their scalding hot black coffee Charlie grabbed hold of his arm and said,

'Well this is it Norman. We are actually going to do it. I must admit that, when we first discussed your plans I was convinced that one or both of us would chicken out, but here we are.'

'Yes here we are,' Norman nodded, once again feeling the gravity of the situation pressing down on him like a heavy weight. But just as soon the mood left him as they discussed their plan to find a base for their operation with all the excitement of a couple of kids planning their first camping trip.

They decided to press on to Membury Services for lunch and set off down the slip road to rejoin the motorway. The van was in its "Landscape Gardeners" mode and looked quite smart. The yellow paint work was nothing like as garish as Norman had imagined it would be. It was more of an Ochre colour and with the dark green panels with their gold sign writing the whole effect was quite tasteful. The van was in remarkably good condition and this had been reflected in its cost. However, Norman had not quibbled and had gladly paid the asking price, having considered all the "extras" and more importantly the speed with which Ginger had accomplished so much. If Ginger had made a few hundred on the deal, so much the better, for although he could certainly do with the money, he was the last bloke in the world to accept a handout.

When they had finished their lunch they drove the eight or so miles to Junction 15 and turned north along the A419 with Swindon to their left as they headed for Cirencester. Now they could start looking for likely places which they could use as their base. Ideally it would be somewhere just off the beaten track preferably with outbuildings large enough to conceal both the van and the car from prying eyes. Another advantage would be a property with two ways in and out. My God, thought Norman as this particular idea flitted through his mind, old Ginger's paranoia must be contagious and he chuckled to himself. Of course they might just spot somewhere that was empty and deserted but that was highly unlikely. They had decided to look around the local estate agents for a property to rent on a short term lease, of hopefully, no more than six months, and even that would take a huge chunk out of the budget.

The long hot spell looked like coming to an

end. The sky was leaden and overcast and the atmosphere had become oppressive. All the signs of an imminent thunder storm and as they passed the outskirts of Cricklade, where the River Thames rises, the first large raindrops splattered onto their dusty windscreens. Norman was pleased to discover that, like everything else on the van, the windscreen washers worked perfectly and were soon clearing away all the road grime and dead insects.

The rain was really bouncing off the road as they negotiated the roundabout into Cirencester and made their way along the narrow street, past the cinema, and into the large car park which appeared to the right of them. They found two adjacent spaces and parked up. They sat and watched the lightning reflecting off the creamy coloured Cotswold stone of the Job Centre building across the road. The ultra bright light seemed to freeze the whole scene momentarily as if someone was taking a gigantic flash photograph of the few figures scurrying to escape the downpour.

It was ten or fifteen minutes before either of them made a move to obtain tickets from the Pay and Display machine, but then there was little danger of any traffic warden checking windscreens for tickets. If they had any sense at all they would be dry and warm in the local nick having a brew.

When the rain stopped and a watery sun had filtered through, casting an eerie light over the town they walked round the corner into Market Place which was dominated by the fine fifteenth century Parish Church of St. John the Baptist. There had been a church on that site since the twelfth century which had originally been served by the priests from the nearby abbey. They went into the Kings Head Hotel in the main street with their minimal luggage and booked a room for a couple of nights.

They rose late on Sunday morning and after a leisurely breakfast they spent a couple of hours strolling around the compact market town and Norman found it hard to believe that this had once been the largest and most important town in the whole of Roman Britain.

The following morning they awoke to see from their bedroom window that, despite the early hour, the market traders had already set up their stalls down the middle of the street on what, the day before, had been a car park. Soon after nine they set off to find an estate agent who specialised in property to let. They were looking ideally for a short term let of a farm property, and at the first agency they visited they struck lucky. The agency had two properties available on short term leases both of which filled most of the criteria they were looking for. Both were farm properties with adequate out buildings and one of them even had two ways in and out albeit a rough track which went through another farm yard but to a different road. The farmer apparently was on a six month fact finding visit to Australia studying methods of sheep farming. He had been a dairy farmer for most of his working life but, like so many lowland farmers, he was contemplating changing over to sheep. He was sick of all the red tape involved with dairy quotas and worries over the BSE scare. He had been away for a month already which meant that the property was available for an incredibly short four month lease. They made an appointment to meet one of the company's sales representatives at this particular farm the same afternoon.

CHAPTER ELEVEN

Back at the hotel Charlie had switched on the television and was watching one of those morning chat shows.

'My God,' she gasped, 'It can't be. It is. It's Samantha. We were at school together during the two years daddy was on some sort of hush hush attachment in darkest Africa. Mummy, Jeremy and I came back to the UK and we both went to boarding school. The former Samantha Lambert was one year ahead of me and I had a terrible crush on her. She was very beautiful and very good at sports. I worshipped her. She is now Lady Samantha Simpkins, wife of Sir Humphrey Simpkins, quite a few years her senior and Under Secretary of State at the Ministry of Transport.'

Norman was only half concentrating on the programme but Lady Samantha seemed to be coming across as a bit of an air head. Her main interest in life seemed to be partying and her husband it appeared, although she never said so in as many words, was a bit of a stuffed shirt. She, from what one could gather, spent most nights out on the town while Sir Humphrey was presumably at home going through his "red boxes".

The interviewer was now asking in a syrupy voice,

'Tell me Samantha, are the rumours I hear about the Detective Inspector in charge of your joint security asking for a transfer correct? The story we hear is that he has had enough of your, quote, wild ways.'

'Yes, I admit that I'm a little impulsive at times. The poor love tries his best to keep up with me, but I do tend to go off at a tangent sometimes. I get bored very quickly and if some of the crowd suddenly decide to shoot off somewhere, I don't always have the time to let him know. My husband is always telling me that someone in my position should act more responsibly, but really. . . I am always on my best behaviour whenever I accompany him to his interminable functions. I sit there for hours on end listening to his political friends droning on and on. . . It drives me absolutely mad. I have to get out sometimes and let my hair down. I know that the Inspector is only trying to do his job, but sometimes he can be an awful bore.'

The two women babbled on for another ten minutes or so and, although Norman didn't think that he was taking much notice, it must have been sinking deep into his sub- conscious. He would remember almost every word of the interview at some time in the future. When the interview had finished, Charlie said,

'She was always kicking over the traces at school. She was almost expelled on more than one occasion for staying out overnight. She is what you might call a Free Spirit and she's certainly a lot of fun to be with. You'd love her Norman.'

'I'm sure that I would,' replied Norman a little frostily,

'But right now, what I would really love would be to get some lunch. We have to be at the farm for one thirty, remember.'

Just before one o clock they set off down the

road towards Swindon and turned off up a narrow side road to Castle Eaton. Through the village they continued uphill for a mile or so and as the road levelled out they saw the farm tucked in amongst the trees. It was nestled in a hollow beyond the hedgerow and as soon as Norman saw it he liked the look of the place. The ground dropped away beyond the buildings and then rose again towards a tree lined ridge three or four miles beyond.

The farmhouse itself was a modest two storey building of Cotswold stone with a slate roof and behind the house they could see two large corrugated asbestos out buildings, and the one nearest the house had what looked like a large water tower placed close to its gable end. The road in front of them dropped slightly and turned slightly to the right concealing the entrance to the farm, so much so, that had they been travelling any faster they would have missed it altogether. That's another plus thought Norman as he stepped on the brakes and turned sharply onto the downhill track.

As they drove slowly down the stony track they saw a red Cavalier. The agent had arrived in advance of them. Norman liked that. He couldn't stand people who were late for appointments. As he stopped the car a young man in a dark grey suit and incongruous green Wellington boots came, hand outstretched, to greet them.

'Roger Green,' he beamed towards Charlie, scarcely giving Norman a cursory glance.

Smooth bastard, thought Norman, as he greeted the salesman brightly. The salesman's wellies were completely superfluous as it turned out and he clumped ahead of them along the well drained track which, despite the previous Saturday's downpour was remarkably dry.

'Shall we start with the house first,' and without waiting for an answer he plunged a long brass coloured Chub key into a sturdy looking lock in the side door which stood back inside a covered porch way. The door opened up on to a large "lived in" looking kitchen which was dominated by a huge well scrubbed table. The kitchen cabinets were of light oak and looked well used although not in the least shabby. On the wall opposite the sink and the large window was the inevitable AGA cooker which provided warmth for the room, more than adequate hot water for the whole house and, of course, four cast iron cooking rings complete with hinged lids together with two large ovens.

The door at the far end of the kitchen led to a very comfortable looking living room which was filled with well stuffed furniture and a marvellous Welsh Dresser which held a very impressive display of, what looked like, genuine Delft ware. The walls were painted plain white and the only relief to that was a selection of old hunting prints and a large fireplace which was constructed from the same stone as the outside of the building. Norman imagined a huge log fire roaring up the chimney on cold winter nights. The rest of the ground floor consisted of the farm office complete with computer, a laundry room and a downstairs toilet and cloakroom. Upstairs they were shown the master bedroom with en-suite facilities and then three smaller bedrooms and the main bathroom. One thing which struck both of them was the quality of the woodwork. All the doors were very substantial and elaborately panelled, and as they were admiring the highly polished wide planks of the landing floor the salesman told them that the owners grandfather who had built the house had, as well as being a farmer, been a very accomplished joiner.

'This all looks great,' enthused Charlie,

'I wouldn't mind living here permanently.'

Norman nodded, and swallowed hard when he considered the asking price for the four months let. It would take a lottery win before he could ever aspire to these standards. And to think farmers were always saying what a hard time they were having . . . the thought made him smile inwardly.

Outside once more they proceeded towards the out buildings. Norman could see, now that they were closer, that what he had taken to be a water tower, was in fact a home-made feed silo.

'Obviously the grandson and present owner of the property has a few skills of his own,' Norman said as he admired the structure. The two large out buildings were very well maintained and easily accessible by means of a wide track of stone chippings. The agent swung open the large double doors of the first building to reveal about a hundred tons of hay baled and stacked neatly at the far end leaving about two thirds of the floor space free. The second building was a modern milking parlour with adjoining indoor accommodation for cattle during the winter months and was of little interest to Norman. The first building would suit his needs admirably.

Norman and Charlie went back into the house again for a final look around before deciding whether or not to rent. Norman went up to one of the smaller bedrooms and stood looking out of the window. It commanded an excellent view of the road along which they had approached the farm. The road going in the other direction was hidden from view by trees and the end of the far outbuilding. That was a slight disadvantage but it couldn't be helped. Anyway the chances were that anyone approaching them would come from the same direction that they themselves had.

He turned to find Charlie had entered the room behind him.

'What do you think?'

'I don't think we'll find anything better,' she said,

'In fact I think that it will be ideal. Did you notice the track running from the back of the cattle-shed. I had a good look and it seems to join the road about a mile further on and looks to be in good repair, just in case we ever need to make a quick exit.,

My God, thought Norman, she must be telepathic or something. He had been thinking exactly the same himself but hadn't actually put his thoughts into words. They really did make a brilliant partnership.

The salesman was stood anxiously looking at his watch as they came down the stairs.

'We'll take it,' and Norman saw a look of smug satisfaction flit across the well shaved pink face. The instant dislike which he had felt for the salesman hadn't diminished yet he couldn't let his personal feelings cock up the deal. As Charlie had said, they would have to look a long way before they found anything better.

The young man produced a rental agreement from his expensive looking brief case and Norman read it carefully before signing it. If he looks at that bloody watch again I'll punch him one Norman thought as he wrote out his cheque for the first month's rent.

CHAPTER TWELVE

As soon as the estate agent had left they locked up the property and set off back to Cirencester. They checked out of the Kings Head and put their luggage into the car. Charlie drove the car having arranged to meet Norman at the large Tesco supermarket by the roundabout on the outskirts of the town. Meanwhile Norman walked round to the car park behind the local cinema. He had moved the van there on the Sunday because they had decided that it would be far less conspicuous at the far end of this parking area.

At the supermarket they bought large amounts

of frozen convenience foods with which to stock the freezer at the farm. This would mean that, whatever time they arrived back from their expeditions, they would be able to prepare a meal quite quickly.

The following morning they both got into the van and Norman backed it out of the barn. They set off towards the main road which would take them up to the M5. Once on the motorway they made good progress north and by ten o clock they were approaching junction 2. They stopped about a quarter of a mile short of the turn off and Charlie climbed into the back of the van and quickly flipped the side panels over so that they read "Motorway Maintenance". Norman donned one of the Day-Glo jackets and a hard hat. He removed one of the explosive devices from its hiding place and an A4 piece of yellow paper which he had sealed in a plastic folder, the kind used for ring binders. He had prepared several of the prints the previous evening on the farms computer. At the top of the sheet, using an elementary graphics package, he had placed the silhouette of a small steam engine . . . the sort used on the old level crossing warning signs. The copy below it read:

F-O-R-B-O-R
Freight Off the Roads
and Back On the Railways

He had been very careful to wear fine rubber gloves when handling the sheets of paper and the plastic bags. As far as knew his fingerprints weren't on record anywhere but he wasn't taking any chances

At last, thought Norman, this was the start of the campaign proper. All the long hours spent in preparation were over. Operation F.O.R.B.O.R. was now finally up and running.

As he got down from the van he grinned at Charlie like a schoolboy about to do a bit of mischief. He strode purposefully to the base of the television tower, confident that he wasn't being monitored. The camera was facing in the opposite direction checking traffic going south on the other carriageway. As he crouched at the foot of the tower he glanced about and to his satisfaction no body was taking the slightest interest in what he was doing. But then he noticed a police Landrover coming up quickly on the inside lane. He held his breath then let it out again with a nervous laugh as the traffic cop in the passenger seat gave him a cheery wave as they sped by.

He placed the little black box on one of the legs of the stanchion and pressed it firmly so that the Plasticine gripped firmly onto the metalwork. He checked once again that it was secure and, before he walked back to the van, he placed the yellow card onto a wooden fencing post by means of a staple gun, being careful to use the gloves again. Charlie was now behind the wheel ready to drive away. Her close cropped hair of a few weeks ago had now grown out and she had it in a smart boyish style. She had also reverted to her own natural blonde colouring and looked absolutely fabulous with her hard hat placed at a cheeky angle. Norman climbed into the passenger seat and she carefully built up speed on the hard shoulder before joining the traffic on the inside lane. Almost as soon as they had joined the stream she was indicating to leave the motorway at the exit to West Bromwich.

They drove around the town and following the signs for Walsall they worked their way north to join the M6 southbound at junction nine. Here they joined a queue of slow moving traffic until they reached the turn off for the M5 south. Slowly the traffic flow picked up and they were moving quite well as they approached junction one. About half a mile before the turn off they stopped on the hard shoulder once again.

Norman hopped out of the van and ran up the three steps which led to the base of another television camera tower. This was also facing oncoming traffic on the other carriageway. He fixed another device to the metalwork and stapled another card onto a tree on the embankment just behind the small elevated platform. Both charges had been placed so that the tower would, barring terribly bad luck, fall away from the carriageway. The object of this exercise was to make the authorities aware of their potential for doing real damage to the road network and to bring their demands to the notice of the Ministry of Transport.

Norman jumped into the back of the van and settled himself so that he could see through the one way glass of the rear windows having quickly removed the radio control with which he would detonate the charges. He was waiting for a break in the traffic on the inside lane and the moment one occurred he signalled to Charlie who pulled out carefully and picked up speed.

When they were about two hundred yards down the road, Norman pressed the button and through the rear window he saw the flash but didn't hear anything because of the articulated lorry which was pounding past them in the middle lane. He did, however, see the mast topple on to the hard shoulder but unfortunately this had caused a maroon Sierra to swerve. It must have been a pure reflex action for the tangled metal work had fallen well within the area of the hard shoulder. The car hit another large truck which was in the second lane. It was only a glancing blow, of which the driver of the truck was not even aware, but it was enough to cause quite a bit of damage to the driver's side of the car and cause him to swerve back across the lane and on to the grass beyond the hard shoulder.

'Shit,' muttered Norman under his breath,

'That wasn't supposed to happen.' It had shaken him and he felt his heart pounding against his ribs. Charlie was driving quite slowly and he was just able to see the driver get out and inspect the damage. No one had been hurt thank God.

Norman had to pull himself together quickly for they were coming up to Junction 2 where the other charge had been placed on the far side of the motorway. Charlie slowed down slightly as they were passing the television mast and Norman pressed the button once more. Again he saw the flash and this time he heard the muffled explosion as they drove on picking up speed cautiously so as not to attract attention to themselves. This time the mast fell well away from the carriageway and there were no incidents this time.

Five or six miles down the motorway they saw three police cars speeding north on the opposite side of the road with lights flashing and sirens screaming.

'YES ! !' Charlie shouted. They were both feeling on a high. The adrenaline was really pumping as they sped along towards Junction 11A were they would turn off for Cirencester and the farm beyond.

'Just keep an eye on the speed,' Norman warned,

'I know just how you feel but the last thing we need now is to be caught speeding.'

Charlie eased her foot from the accelerator in response to the warning and she turned her head slightly towards Norman in the back of the van looking slightly flushed and said,

'I'll have to pull off at Strensham. I'm absolutely bursting for a wee. It must be all the excitement. By the way did I tell you? I'm not wearing anything under these overalls. And when I've been to the loo I'll show you some real excitement. As soon as I stop you get those floor boards up and we'll make use of the mattress the sergeant kindly installed for us. I don't know about you but I'm feeling very randy.'

Norman was feeling the same way and was already getting the back of the van ready as she drove up the slip road into the service area. She parked close to the toilets and jumped out almost before the van had stopped. Two or three minutes later she was back in the driver's seat and she pulled across to the far side of the car park well away from any other vehicles.

It had started raining now as she jumped out of the van and ran round to the back doors. By the time she had climbed into the van and closed the doors behind her she had already unzipped the front of her overalls. She knelt with her knees either side of Norman who had already removed everything apart from his boxer shorts. She reached down, released his rock hard erection and watched it disappear as she took its whole length into her hot, throbbing wetness. The events of the morning must really have turned her on. Norman had never seen anyone so wild during love making. She seemed absolutely insatiable and he was completely exhausted by the time she had finished and had finally collapsed on top of him after yet another series of noisy, shuddering orgasms.

It was perhaps as well the van was parked well away from any of the other vehicles as it bounced up and down flexing its suspension to the maximum. The pair inside however had been completely oblivious to anything or anyone as the rain had pounded down on the metal roof above them.

CHAPTER THIRTEEN

The three Traffic cars arrived at the scene of the second explosion almost simultaneously. All six occupants jumped out and started running about doing what Traffic cops do best . . . placing lines of cones everywhere and waving all the traffic into one outside lane. Of course this would have exactly the opposite effect to that which the powers that be would have wished for. A single line of slow moving vehicles, their drivers having plenty of time to inspect the fallen television camera mast. They had only just realised that the mast had probably been toppled by some sort of explosive device rather than by something having crashed into it. In fairness that would be the first conclusion reached by any Traffic patrol were it not for the absence of any skid marks or for that matter any damaged vehicle at the scene.

Fortunately, whilst they were busy deploying long lines of cones and directing the traffic away from the inside lanes, an Inspector from the Regional Crime Squad was approaching the scene. He drove through a gap in the cones and along the hard shoulder towards the spot where the mast lay. An archetypal Traffic cop with his slashed peaked cap, small dark moustache, sunglasses (despite the fact that it had already started to drizzle) and day-glow jacket waved him down furiously and stuck his head aggressively through the Inspectors window.

'Where do you think you're going sunshine?' he said officiously.

'Inspector Deakin, Regional Crime Squad,' and he pushed his identity folder into the man's face.

'Sorry Sir,' he said rather reluctantly and then he proceeded to give the Inspector his theory of what had occurred.

'Thank you, constable,' he cut him off in full flow.

Deakin parked his car and was strolling over to the mangled stump of the mast when he noticed the yellow sign pinned to the fence beyond it. He went back to his car and put on a pair of rubber surgical gloves and took out a large plastic evidence bag.

'Has anyone touched that sign over there constable?'

'Don't know Sir, don't think so.'

Surly bastard, thought the Inspector, as he walked over to the fence. He carefully removed the sign being careful to remove the staples with which it was attached. He bagged it and placed a label on the bag showing the time, date and location of the evidence and locked it in his car boot ready to hand over to forensics. He then took out his mobile phone and called the headquarters of West Midlands Police force.

'Commander Duncan, Anti Terrorist Squad,' he said after identifying himself.

There was a slight pause and then a gravelly voice boomed out of the earpiece,

'Duncan, what's the problem?'

'Detective Inspector Deakin, Regional Crime Squad, Sir. I though you ought to know. It looks as though there has been an explosion close to Junction 2 on the M5 north bound. A television monitoring mast down. Thought you'd want your people here before too many pairs of feet start trampling around.'

'Good work Inspector. Keep the area as clear as you can. Get Traffic to help you. No doubt the place is swarming with them already.'

'Yes Sir, will do.'

Almost before he had slammed down the receiver, Duncan was pressing a button on his desk. A pretty detective constable came into the room carrying her note pad.

'Sir?'

'Get Chief Superintendent Laidlow and that new side kick of his in here as soon as possible.'

'Right away Sir, and Oh, I don't know whether it concerns us or not, but Traffic Surveillance are reporting that two of their monitoring cameras on the M5 have gone down within five minutes of each other. One northbound and one southbound.'

'Thank you Constable, Mr. Laidlow as soon as you can please.'

Two cameras down. That sounds ominous, especially in view of the last phone call, he thought, and he picked up the phone again.

'Get me Traffic. . . Inspector Jenkins,' a brief pause and then,

'Hello Jack, Jim Duncan here, how's things? Tell me Jack, have you had any incidents reported on the M5 south bound around Junction 1 during the last hour or so?''

'Just the one Sir. The driver of a maroon Sierra hit a lorry a glancing blow and is now pulled up on the hard shoulder talking to our lads. He's a bit shaken up but says he saw, now wait for this, a television mast falling over and it caused him to swerve. He has been breathalysed of course but there's no problem on that score so one of the crew is walking back up the hard shoulder to investigate. Incidentally, the pictures from that and one other camera have gone down, I've just been informed. Could be connected.'

'Thanks a lot Jack. Keep me posted.'

There was a tap on the door and Chief Superintendent Laidlow ambled in closely followed by Detective Sergeant Newman.

Laidlow was in his late fifties and had been round the block a time or two. He had started out in the Met' in 1956 shortly after completing his National Service, most of which was spent at RAF Kai Tak where he served with the S.P.'s, the Air Force equivalent of the Military Police.

When he was demobbed it was a toss-up between the Hong Kong Police force or the

Metropolitan force of his native London. The Met' won and Bill Laidlow had made the rank of Sergeant within three years of joining. He was a good old fashioned copper with a "nose" for the job. He had risen swiftly through the ranks, a lot quicker than he would have done in the present climate, bogged down with PACE and all the other political correctness which worked so much in favour of the villains. He was regarded in some circles as something of a dinosaur, but his vast experience over the years in the Flying Squad, Special Branch, and more recently his sterling service with the Anti Terrorist Squad, which included several stints in Northern Ireland, had made his position fairly unassailable.

To look at Bill Laidlow sat there in his well worn tweed jacket sucking on his ancient briar pipe he gave the impression of being a kindly old grandad, but anyone who ever had crossed swords with him would give you quite a different description. He could be ruthless, even down right brutal in his quest to bring wrong doers to justice. There weren't many unsolved cases in Laidlow's pending tray.

Detective Sergeant Martin Newman, on the

other hand, was one of the new school. Public school in fact, then on to University and the Police College at Hendon. After passing out with flying colours he spent just twelve months at Cannon Row and he had been made up to Sergeant. He was then seconded to the Anti Terrorist Squad and placed under the very experienced wing of Bill Laidlow. He stood erect, resplendent in his dark blue Chester Barrie suit in complete contrast to his superior who was slumped in one of the well worn leather arm chairs in the Commanders office.

'Do sit down Sergeant,' said the Commander testily,

'You make me feel uncomfortable standing there as if you had a broom stick stuck up your arse.'

Newman coloured slightly and selected a rigid plastic chair and sat at attention next to Laidlow. Typical bloody public school type thought Duncan as he spread his huge hairy hands on the desk before him.

'It looks like we've had a couple of small explosions on the M5 just before lunch this morning. Nothing major, no casualties but just as a precaution Traffic have been instructed to seal off the M6 from Junction 9 South to the M5 turn off and the M5 from Junction 3 North. I want you two down there pronto. Start at the site of the second explosion just south of Junction 2. I've asked an Inspector Deakin of the Regional Crime Squad to wait for you. Fortunately he happened on the scene shortly after the lads from Traffic and he is doing his best to keep the site sterile as far as he can. Forensics and the local Bomb Disposal Crew have been notified.

'Any claims been made yet Sir?'

Laidlow was re-lighting his pipe and blowing out thick clouds of smoke, most of which drifted towards Newman. The young sergeant coughed and wafted the smoke away but Laidlow pretended not to notice. He just smiled inwardly.

'No, Nothing yet,' replied the Commander,

'But somehow I've got a feeling that this is nothing to do with our Irish friends. Nothing specific you understand, merely a gut feeling.'

Laidlow and Newman arrived at the scene less than an hour after the second explosion. Inspector Deakin had done a good job and had already got the area cordoned off with blue and white plastic "POLICE" tape. He reported what he had found and handed the evidence bag over to Laidlow.

'I really must be on my way now Superintendent, if that's OK with you. I'm already over an hour late for an interview with an inmate of Winson Green prison. Not that he is likely to be going anywhere for the next ten years or so but I'd like to get over there Sir.'

'Thanks very much for your help Inspector,' said Laidlow puffing contentedly on his old pipe.

'You've done an excellent job here and I'll see to it that your superiors are informed. It never hurts to build up a few "Brownie Points" in this job. Just one thing before you go Inspector and this is very important. I don't want any mention of that poster which you have just passed on to me in your report. I cannot stress the importance of this enough. I will also be instructing the boys from Traffic to keep a lid on this information. I'll threaten them with confiscation of their fast, shiny, noisy toys. The only thing they will ever drive again is a desk if they say anything to anyone.'

Saying that he lifted the plastic tape allowing Deakin to drive off to his appointment.

The bomb disposal people had been sent in, although, at this point it seemed unlikely that there were any more unexploded devices in the vicinity, but caution was always the watchword in these cases. The Motorways had now been sealed off from Junction 3 northwards on the M5 and from Junction 10 southwards on the M6. The traffic jams around the west of Birmingham were horrendous.

Just then Newman's mobile phone rang.

'It's for you Sir,'

Laidlow refused to carry one of these "yuppie toys" much to the amusement of his younger colleagues.

'Duncan here, Superintendent, it seems that there has been another explosion on the southbound carriageway. Traffic are on the scene at the moment. Get young Newman up there ASAP before any of the evidence is disturbed.'

'Right away Sir' but the connection had already been severed.

'Sergeant, get on the radio and get a Traffic car to come down the other carriageway and take you back up to the site of the other explosion. If there is another of the yellow posters there, get it under wraps immediately. I have decided to sit on them for the time being. I have never heard of this FORBOR lot before and I don't want any press speculation at this stage. We'll just let them make up their own story. They usually do that anyway. I should think that by the six o clock news this evening we will definitely be looking at yet another IRA outrage.

The heavy rain of an hour previous had passed over now and the sun was already drying the road surface. Sergeant Newman jumped down from the Landrover and ran up the three steps at the base of the fallen television mast. There, sure enough, pinned to the trunk of a tree behind the small enclosure was another yellow notice, similar to the one found at the other site. He repeated Laidlow's warning about the notice complete with all the threats about driving a desk and losing their fast shiny toys. They had got the message loud and clear.

'What notice was that?' one of them was saying as he made his way back to his Landrover.

CHAPTER FOURTEEN

They arrived back at the farm at about two in the afternoon. Norman had driven from Strensham and Charlie had been particularly quiet throughout the journey. She had hopped out of the van as soon as they reached the farmhouse and Norman had carried on round to the barn to park the van.

'I'll put the kettle on,' she said as she got out and hurried into the house. Norman was puzzled by her mood and began to torture himself with the thought that he may have proved a disappointment to her back at the car park.

He had just parked the van and was locking the two large double doors of the barn when it started to rain again. He rushed back to the house and stood there dripping all over the kitchen floor. Charlie looked up from the teapot and smiled sheepishly,

'You'd better get out of that lot and get into something dry.'

Norman nodded and did as she suggested. He came back down into the large comfortable living room where Charlie was already curled up in one of the well padded armchairs cradling her mug of tea in both hands.

They both opened their mouths to speak at the same moment and Norman held out his hand towards her,

'You first.'

'I don't know quite what to say,' she started quietly,

'You must be absolutely appalled by my behaviour back there in the car park. I honestly don't know what came over me. I acted like some wanton slut. You were shocked weren't you. I shocked myself.'

'You were absolutely bloody magnificent. It was probably the excitement of the morning's events. I felt quite turned on myself,' beamed Norman feeling quite relieved.

'Mind you, I don't think that I could take that sort of treatment too often. I think that I would soon become a total physical wreck.'

'Don't worry, I'll be gentle with you tonight,' she whispered, and with that they both dissolved into fits of laughter. The awkwardness had completely disappeared.

They both sat there with their mugs of tea watching the rain beating against the window panes, not saying a word, just easy in each other's company. They sat like that for an hour or so until Norman decided it was time for food. Neither of them had eaten since breakfast.

He went through to the kitchen and called back,

'Fancy a pizza?'

'Sounds fine,' Charlie replied and half an hour later they were sat in front of the television with half a large pizza each together with a tossed salad and large glass of Chianti. The news was just starting.

'Large areas of the West Midlands were grid locked with heavy traffic following the closure of parts of the M5 and M6 motorways.'

The picture cut from the news reader to a large roundabout which could have been in any large conurbation anywhere in the country. The shot was obviously taken from a helicopter and as the camera panned around there was solid traffic stretching for miles in every direction. The voice over continued in that blasé,, matter of fact voice that news readers work so hard to perfect,

'A spokesman for West Midlands Police Force said earlier that two small explosive devices had been detonated close the North and South bound carriage ways of the M5. The Anti Terrorist Squad and bomb disposal experts are still at the scene and, as yet, no one has claimed responsibility for the incidents which are believed to have happened around mid day. The motorways have now been re opened but it will be some hours before traffic in the Midlands finally gets back to normal . . .

The Chancellor of the Exchequer announced further plans today . . .'

'What a load of bollocks,' cried Norman indignantly,

'What the hell are they talking about? No one has claimed responsibility. You saw me staple those notices to the fence and the tree. What the bloody hell are they playing at?'

Norman had now abandoned his plate and placed it on the floor beside his chair. He took a long swig of his wine and lapsed into seething silence. He was furious.

'Calm down Norman,' Charlie soothed as she continued to eat her meal.

'It's no good getting all worked up. I suspect the police haven't released all the details to the media yet. There will be more on the later bulletin I'm sure.'

Norman wasn't completely convinced.

'I don't like it. They will probably say nothing about our claims and everyone will just assume, as usual, that it's down to those crazy Irish bastards again. All that bloody work for nothing. Well I'll show them. We'll show them. Next time we will really give them something to think about. No more pussy footing around.'

'Here finish your meal,' Charlie picked up the plate from the floor and then poured him another large glass of wine. Norman pushed the food around his plate with a sullen look on his face.

'Why would they conceal the fact that they had found our messages? I just don't understand it.'

Charlie had finished her pizza and was disappearing into the kitchen.

'Coffee?' she said over her shoulder as she went.

'Cheer up love. I'll bet anything you like that there will be more details revealed on the late news.'

Love? Had she just called him love? Norman cheered up considerably as they washed and dried the few pots which they had just used. The sun was out again now and they decided to walk over the hill and down into the village. They spent a pleasant hour or so on one of the benches outside the pub enjoying a pint of the particularly good local beer and watching the world go by. It was a lovely evening and the setting sun was painting fantastic orange and pink shapes in the sky as they walked hand in hand back over the hill to the farm.

It was just before ten as they got back and as Norman switched on the television the familiar chimes of News at Ten were just ringing out. The closing of the Motorways was still the lead story and they were showing some of the ensuing congestion again. They went on to reveal that two traffic surveillance cameras had been toppled by small explosive devices but they were still maintaining that no one had claimed responsibility.

'What the hell are they playing at,' Norman exploded.

'I'm going to ring ITN and tell them just why those explosions happened. I'll give them a follow up. If I ring now they will probably get it on by the end of the programme.'

'Just listen to yourself,' Charlie sounded exasperated.

'That would be a really smart move wouldn't it. You DO realise, don't you, just how easy it is to trace a call these days. Dial 1471 and you get the information instantaneously. None of that old nonsense of keeping the call short like they did in the old movies. My God, the police would be pounding on the door ten minutes after you replaced the receiver.'

'I know, I know you're right Charlie, but we have to do something. We can't just sit around doing nothing. We have to make sure that our demands are made public.'

Charlie leaned over the back of his chair and ran her fingers through his hair.

'Let's sleep on it,' she whispered,

'I promised to be gentle with you tonight, remember?'

But Norman wasn't in the mood. He sat there staring at the television without really seeing it. It was just a background babble to his racing thoughts.

'Oh very well then,' Charlie pouted.

'You just sit there and sulk all night. I'm going up,' and with that she swept out of the room towards the staircase. She undressed and lay on the bed feeling sure that he would follow her up soon, but when he didn't appear she pulled the duvet over her head and lay there thinking. Slowly the nucleus of an alternative idea was forming in her head. When Norman finally came up to bed she feigned sleep but her mind was still working overtime. She had decided to enlist the help of Ginger Robson and that would mean making a phone call without Norman knowing about it. She wasn't going to tell him about her plan for the time being. She wanted to discuss it's feasibility with Ginger first. She would just go along with the explosives campaign for the time being and do her best to keep a rein of Norman's anger and frustration.

When she woke up the following morning Norman was already up. She went downstairs calling his name but there was no reply. Oh, God I hope he hasn't decided to do anything stupid she thought as she dashed back up to the bedroom to get dressed. She quickly pulled on a pair of jeans and a sweat shirt and hurried down to the barn to check if the two vehicles were still there.

As she pushed open one of the large doors she saw to her relief that they were and then she saw Norman also dressed in jeans. He was moving bales of hay.

'Morning,' she shouted cheerfully,

'What are you up to?'

'I felt like a work out when I got up this morning. I've been missing my twice weekly visits to the gym this last few weeks so I thought I would try getting back in shape. I thought that I may as well do something useful while I'm at it. I have decided to move the first three rows of bales forward by ten or fifteen feet. Well about two thirds of the first three rows that is. I thought it might be a good idea to run the car and the van behind them. It might be useful at some time in the future if anyone decides to start poking around.'

'Good idea,' she said, relieved that he wasn't chasing off half cocked and doing something rash. Something that they may both regret later.

'Would you mind if I borrowed the car this morning? I want to go into Swindon or Cirencester. I need to pick some girlie things up from Boots.'

'Sure. No problem,' said Norman throwing her the ignition keys. He didn't want to get into any discussion about "girlie" things.

Great, thought Charlie. That was a lot easier than I thought it would be. Now she would be able to contact Ginger and take her time telling him about her plan without being overheard. She would, incidentally have a few items of shopping to buy. Items which she would have to hide from Norman for the time being and that wouldn't be too difficult. She smiled to herself. Norman, considering that he had been married for years, was strangely reticent when it came to female matters. She had noticed how he had coloured slightly when she mentioned the nature of her shopping trip.

CHAPTER FIFTEEN

Superintendent Laidlow was slumped comfortably in his well worn office chair as Newman walked in.

'Anything back yet from forensics on the "FORBOR" notices Sergeant?' he said slowly tamping some fresh tobacco into his pipe.

'Not a great deal to go on yet Sir. There are no fingerprints on either the paper or the plastic folders. It would appear that surgical gloves were used both in preparing the notices and during the placing of them at the scene of the explosions. The paper is a very common brand of copier paper. According to the report it is 70gsm Bond - colour "Old Gold", trade name

"Premium Copier Paper". A brand which is sold by two of the leading Office Supplies companies who have outlets on almost every retail park in the country. Apparently if we can find the wrapper in which it was packed, the batch number would tell us the actual store where it was sold. The plastic wallets are also a very common brand which is sold by the same outlets and the same proviso regarding the packaging applies. The notices were printed from mid range PC via a fairly good quality 600 dpi printer. The report lists four possibilities.'

'Thank you Sergeant. Suppose we work on the probability that the paper and the plastic folders were bought at the same time. Not an unreasonable proposition you will agree. Get a check under way on all the major office supply companies within a hundred miles radius of the explosions. Computerised till records will no doubt throw up the probabilities but computers have their limitations. I much prefer to rely on the human brain. If any likely purchases are thrown up I want you to go and interview the sales staff personally. It never fails to amaze me just what is stored in the memory of the average person. Over half of the information is stored without the person even realising it and often it takes only the slightest stimulation to reveal a crucial piece of information.'

'I'll get onto that straight away Sir, but just before I go I should tell you that the report from the bomb disposal people isn't any more encouraging. What few fragments have been recovered lead to the conclusion that the devices were constructed from common, easy to obtain materials. The main body of the devices, which appear to have been quite compact, were probably similar in size to an audio tape cassette holder and made of the same type of black plastic. The explosive was Semtex which isn't quite so easily available but unfortunately not uncommon and extremely difficult to trace due to the fact that most of it comes into the country illegally from former Eastern Bloc countries. The electrical components were far too damaged for any positive identification to be made. However they do add that whoever constructed these devices definitely knows what he is doing. We may well be looking at ex army.'

Sergeant Newman would have some success in tracing the purchaser of the paper and plastic folders. When Norman and Charlie were driving around Swindon on their way up from London, Norman suddenly realised that they would need to plant some sort of message at the scene of the explosions they were planning. They would require some materials with which to make those messages and it just happened that they were passing one of the large retail parks which are to be found on the outskirts of most large towns. He had indicated too turn left off the main road and Charlie followed him into the car park of Office World. She parked alongside him and opened the van door with a puzzled look on her face. Norman explained about the notices he wanted to prepare and asked her to buy some brightly coloured A4 paper, some plastic wallets and a couple of the largest "Jumbo" felt tip markers she could find. She went into the store and found that the A4 paper was only available in packets of a ream (500 sheets) which seemed rather a lot for what they would require but when she saw the price she decided that it wasn't such an extravagant purchase. The plastic wallets were packaged in twenty fives and the selection of felt tip markers was amazing. She selected a large red and an even larger black one of these. She didn't really take much notice of the sales girl at the till. She was quick and efficient and had a pleasant smile but had anyone asked Charlie, ten minutes later, to describe her she wouldn't have had a clue.

However had anyone asked Irene Matthews, the sales girl, to describe Charlie hours, or even days later she would have been able to describe her in quite some detail. Irene, a very smart thirty year old single lady was very interested in young girls like Charlie. She was "gay" but not overtly so. Her employers had no idea of her sexual preferences because, wisely, she never let those preferences surface in the workplace. As far as the store was concerned she was a very efficient, well respected member of staff.

When Newman had contacted the Stationery Stores and had asked them for information about the purchase of the paper and the folders he had expected to wait for days before receiving any information. In the event the suppliers were very cooperative and within twenty four hours he had received replies from almost every one he had contacted. There were only three instances of the particular brand of paper and plastic folders occurring on the same transaction. One in Stoke-on-Trent, one in

Wolverhampton and one in Swindon.

He tried the Wolverhampton store first, that being the closest to the office. He interviewed a very nervous young man who was suffering from what looked like terminal acne and got absolutely nowhere. The lad couldn't even remember the transaction let alone whether the purchaser was male or female, young or old. He had no more success in Stoke-on-Trent and he came away from the store wondering if, in fairness, he would have done any better, after all there must be hundreds of customers a day passing through those tills.

As it was almost five o clock and he was now in the middle of the rush hour traffic, he decided to leave Swindon until the following morning and in the light of events he wasn't very optimistic.

He arrived at the retail park in Swindon just after nine and asked for the manager who asked his secretary to put out a call for the sales assistant who had processed the transaction in question.

'There's a room just across the corridor which you can use Sergeant,' he said cheerfully.

Newman thanked him and he followed Irene

Matthews into the smaller office.

'Please, sit down,' he said, indicating the chair at the other side of the desk.

'I know this is asking rather a lot Miss Mathews, but quite frankly we are grasping at straws in an investigation which we are currently carrying out. I assume the manager has told you of the purchase we are interested in.'

'Yes,' replied the girl, 'As a matter of fact I do remember the purchase. The items were bought by a young blonde girl. Very attractive she was. Short cropped blonde hair and a good figure. She was wearing jeans and a peachy coloured crop top. It was late on last Saturday afternoon. I remember that it rained quite heavily that afternoon.'

'Really,' said Newman rather sceptically.

'Tell me, why do you remember that transaction in particular. I should imagine that this place is quite busy on a Saturday. So why this particular girl.'

'Well Sergeant,' she replied with mischievous grin,

'Let me put it this way. You are quite a presentable looking young man but I'm afraid I wouldn't have remembered much about you ten

146

minutes after you left.'

Newman looked a little perplexed and she said,

'Nothing personal. I'm sure you understand.'

Newman blushed slightly,

'Oh, I see. I'm sorry. I didn't mean . . . I mean your personal preferences are none of my business.'

Newman had not yet become fully used to interviewing people. He still got quite embarrassed and often wondered, at times like this, whether or not he had made the right choice when he had decided to join the police force. His father, a very successful barrister, had been absolutely appalled when he told him that he intended to become a policeman. He still felt uncomfortable when he remembered his father's reaction. When he had come down from Oxford having graduated with honours to gain his Ll.B., his father had naturally assumed that he would join the highly lucrative family practice.

'I've embarrassed you haven't I Sergeant. I'm sorry. I'd like to ask you a favour please. My employers don't have to know do they? I really like my job here. I know that the company would honour the "Equal Opportunities" legislation but I just don't want the hassle.'

'No of course not Irene. I may call you Irene? No I'll just tell them that you could vaguely remember the sale but not much about the person concerned. After all it was very busy wasn't it. I'll not take up any more of your time and thanks again, you have been most helpful.'

'Oh just one more thing Sergeant. She works for a firm of landscape gardeners. I just happened to notice the side of the van as she pulled away.' What the girl hadn't seen was Charlie getting out of the van and getting into the car before driving off.

He was still rather surprised at the detail which Irene Mathews had remembered. He wondered if it would be of much use in their investigation. The girl probably had nothing at all to do with the explosions but, on the other hand, this may be a small but crucial part of the jigsaw.

Driving back up the A419 towards Cirencester and the M5 he would have been more than a little surprised to know that he had actually passed Charlie going in the opposite direction.

CHAPTER SIXTEEN

Charlie parked the car in the multi storey car park above the shopping mall and hurried down to find a telephone kiosk. She was hoping to catch Ginger before he went out. She dialled the number which quickly started to ring out in Sussex Gardens.

'Hello,' the surly voice of Mrs. Whatsit boomed out of the earpiece.

'Hello,' replied Charlie cheerfully. She could just imagine Mrs. Whatsit standing there in the hallway in her cross over pinafore and wearing her usual scowl.

'Is that the Radner Private Hotel?'

Her enquiry was met by a curt yes.

'Would it be possible to speak to Mr. Robson please.'

'No, he left just over a week ago. Who's asking?'

Oh, blast, Charlie thought.

'Charlotte Forbes-Smythe here. Did Mr. Robson leave a forwarding address by any chance?'

'No he didn't, but he said if you or your friend rang I was to give you his mobile phone number.'

Charlie could hear the disapproval in her voice as she read out the number.

'Many thanks,' said Charlie politely and she replaced the phone. She reached into her large shoulder bag and pulled out a handful of change for her next call. She dialled the mobile number. It rang out for quite some time before Ginger finally answered.

'Robson.'

'Hi Ginger, it's Charlie.'

'Sorry hen. It's a bit awkward just now. Can I phone you later.'

'It's rather difficult Ginger. I'm in a call box and I don't have a permanent number at the moment,' she lied.

'Can I call you later?'

'Are you all right lassie? Is Norman with you?'

'I'm absolutely fine Ginger. I just want to have a private word with you and I don't want

Norman to know about it for the time being.'

'Call me back in an hour,' Ginger sounded preoccupied. He was probably in the middle of some shady deal. Charlie set off round the shops. Killing an hour in a shopping mall was never a problem. The generous allowance which her father had set up for her had continued even after his death, obviously perpetuated in his will. Consequently she still enjoyed the advantages of her "Gold" credit card. She went into Boots first and purchased a few personal items. Norman would be very suspicious he she returned without a chemist's carrier bag. Next she visited Marks & Spencer where she bought half a dozen pairs of plain white cotton briefs. Then onto a large DIY store to purchase two pairs of medium sized disposable overalls. She spent the rest of the hour browsing in a couple of small exclusive boutiques and by the end of the hour she had two more carrier bags. One contained a lime green mini dress with a very finely pleated skirt and the other held a pair of strappy sandals in a slightly darker contrasting shade of green.

As she approached the bank of telephone kiosks she spotted something out of the corner of eye. It was a skimpy little bikini in the window of "Knicker Box". It was almost exactly the same shade of green as the sandals she had just bought. She couldn't resist. The top was virtually useless as a bra but the skimpy lycra briefs would be ideal under her new dress.

By the time she dialled Ginger's number again just over an hour and a quarter had elapsed.

'I was beginning to get worried lassie,' Ginger said with genuine concern.

'Sorry Ginger. Once I start shopping I lose all track of time,' she apologised.

'Anyway to get to the point, I would like you to keep tabs on someone for me for a day or two. But before I give you a name I want you to give me your honest opinion. Our first foray into blowing things up wasn't an outstanding success.'

'Was that little item on the M5 yesterday down to you two by any chance,' Ginger interrupted.

'Yes it was and as you will have gathered from the news bulletins they are not saying anything about our demands. Norman is very angry and frustrated. Anyway I have the nucleus of an idea which may prove a much more effective way of getting our demands taken seriously. Now be honest Ginger; just how feasible would it be to abduct someone. Someone fairly high profile. Someone who warrants police protection but often kicks over the traces by shaking off her escort.'

'Do I presume that we are talking about the wife of the Under Secretary of State for Transport?'

'My God Ginger. How the hell did you deduce that?'

Charlie was appalled. Was it so bloody obvious.

'You're not the only one to watch the morning chat shows hen. It was just a good guess, having watched Lady Samantha the other morning. Let me keep tabs on her for a few days as you suggest and I'll let you know. Where can I reach you?'

'Don't ring me Ginger. I'll contact you on your mobile in a couple of days for a progress report. I don't want to raise any false hopes for Norman just yet. Are you alright for money by the way? I can arrange for funds to be deposited in your bank account if you give me the number.'

'Forget the money for now. In my line of business you don't have bank accounts. They tend to make things far too traceable for comfort. If I have anything positive to report perhaps we can meet up somewhere and discuss the matter. Ring me on Saturday morning if you can get away, if not Sunday morning. You can tell old "Nosey" that you're going to church,' he said with a chuckle.

'OK, thanks a lot Ginger. Till Saturday then. Bye.'

Before she returned to the car park she used her "Gold" card once more. She purchased a very compact mobile phone. It would be far easier to slip into the barn or somewhere else around the farm to make a call than making excuses about shopping trips into town. She made another phone call to Ginger to tell him her new mobile number but she made it very clear that the number was only to be used in an absolute emergency.

As she drove out of town towards the A419 she was thinking about Samantha Lambert. To say that she had been at school with her wasn't exactly true. She had been at the same school at the same time. She had been a year below

Samantha and had held her in awe. Samantha was a very attractive and vivacious girl. Her most prominent feature was her beautiful auburn hair which was shoulder length and often tied up into a "pony tail". She had the most fantastic green eyes which stared out of a perfectly smooth complexion. Her figure was superb. She was very athletic but by no means muscular. She excelled at every game and always wore the shortest games skirts. Boys from the nearby comprehensive school would climb the stone wall which surrounded the well manicured sports field of Queensbridge and drool whenever she stooped to pick up a ball or reached high to serve on the tennis court. Charlie had been entranced by her from the first time she saw her. One of the highlights of her time at Queensbridge had been the time she had been invited to play for the first team at net ball. Sickness had depleted the team and the games mistress, who knew that she had proved her self during internal "House" matches, had selected her for the match against one of the school's most dreaded opponents.

When they had boarded the coach to take them to the match Samantha, their captain, had taken Charlie under her wing. She had sat next to her during the journey and Charlie had enjoyed the close contact as their thighs came into contact on the cramped seat of the mini-coach. They won the match and the girls were in high spirits as they went back into the changing rooms and headed for the showers. Charlie had found herself staring at Samantha in the communal shower and had blushed uncontrollably when their eyes had met. She had never had feelings like this before, not even for a boy and it worried her that she might have lesbian tendencies. She soon realised however that her only tendency at that moment was envy. Samantha had a body to die for. Unusually, for one of her hair colouring, she had a lovely all over tan. All over apart from a little white triangle around the neatly trimmed hair of her "bikini line". She had obviously enjoyed many holidays abroad and had gone topless when she sun bathed. She had long well shaped legs, a flat, almost concave, tummy and large firm breasts. She laughed across the steamy room and, after a short embarrassed pause, Charlie laughed back. After the game they had enjoyed afternoon tea in the school refectory and then

Samantha had, with one of her devastating smiles, persuaded the mini-coach driver to take them into the local town for an hour. They had enjoyed a couple of drinks in one of the pubs and Samantha had rounded them up saying that they didn't want to get the driver into trouble by being late back at Queensbridge. It was so typical of her, organising a couple of celebratory drinks for the girls, yet concerned that the driver shouldn't get into any strife. All in all Samantha was quite a remarkable girl. Little surprise that she had done so well for herself married now to a Knight of the realm no less.

When Charlie arrived back at the farm Norman was still in the barn. He was sat on a bale of straw with a can of lager in his hand. She was amazed to see that he had moved over half of the bales already.

'You must be absolutely exhausted,' she said,

'Don't you over do it. You haven't exercised for weeks and now you throw yourself into this lot like there's no tomorrow. Just take it easy for God's sake. I don't want you having a bloody heart attack on me. I know you are frustrated about yesterday but please, take it easy.'

'I've decided that we'll have another go later

on today. I thought later this evening when the light is fading and there isn't quite so much traffic on the move. I want us to try something a bit more ambitious this time. Probably an overhead gantry. Something that will take a bit of clearing up. What do you think?'

'I think it's a good idea Norman. Whereabouts were you thinking of. How about the M5, M4 junction. Perhaps we could leave it until Thursday evening. That way we could cause havoc with the Friday holiday traffic to the West Country. It's the height of the season now.'

She was playing for time. She didn't want him going off half-cocked in his present state of mind.

'OK, Thursday evening it is then. Gives us a chance to have a run down there in the car tomorrow and select a target.'

He helped her with her carrier bags into the house.

Been on a bit of a spending spree have we. Bought anything interesting?'

Charlie knew very well what he meant by anything interesting and said with a provocative grin,

'We'll just have to wait and see won't we. If you are very good I may show you later,' and with that she took the bags and disappeared up the stairs.

CHAPTER SEVENTEEN

Ginger Robson was sitting well down in the seat of a dark green Vauxhall Astra. It was just after seven thirty on Thursday morning and he was parked in Chester Row watching a large house which was just visible round the corner in Eaton Place. It was a large, well maintained town house, the home of Sir Humphrey and Lady Simpkins. Ginger had to be very careful in an area like this and that was why he was wearing a dark blue business suit and why he had borrowed a late model car from one of his many friends in the motor trade. Had he turned up in his old Sierra dressed in his normal attire it would only have been a matter of an hour or so before he was challenged either by one of the regular beat bobbies or by one of the residents themselves. The people who lived in this locality were well connected, old money and were very keen to preserve the exclusivity of the neighbourhood.

Inside the house on Eaton Place, Samantha was packing a mauve coloured sports bag bearing the logo of Vanderbilt perfume ready for her morning visit to an exclusive gym down by the river in Chelsea. Her husband was ensconced behind his copy of the Times having enjoyed a large traditional English breakfast and his man, Matthews, was pouring him a second cup of dark roast Colombian coffee. Samantha breezed into the morning room, kissed him on the forehead and sat down on the opposite side of the table.

'The usual please, Matthews.'

The usual consisted of a large bowl of muesli with un-skimmed milk topped with spoonful of plain organic yogurt followed by a small glass of freshly squeezed orange juice.

'Anything interesting in there darling? Any juicy gossip I ought to know about before I meet the girls at the gym?'

Sir Humphrey answered with a stifled grunt. It was a routine they went through on the rare occasions they met over the breakfast table.

'Whilst I've got you sat down Humphrey, you

won't forget that we are going down to Queensbridge tomorrow evening for the Prize Day. Please try not to get bogged down with any boring cabinet meetings. You know how much I'm looking forward to presenting the prizes. It's a great honour for any old girl of the school to be asked. I will, of course, go by myself if it is absolutely necessary but I would really like you to be there. It won't be too boring for you, there is the Annual Ball afterwards and after we have led off the first dance I feel sure that you will meet someone influential among the fathers. You'll like that won't you darling.'

'And I suppose that you will no doubt find someone's interesting elder brother with whom to dance the night away DARLING,' he replied acidly.

Too bloody right I will she thought with a large grin on her face. Humphrey carried on with his newspaper totally unconcerned. He had become used to his wife's behaviour and although he didn't approve he was content to put up with it just so long as there was no scandal which would affect his career. Her little indiscretions were worth putting up with. She was a marvellous hostess when he needed her to be and he was always amused when he saw the envious looks on the faces of his colleagues when she was on his arm. She really was a stunner. Samantha downed her glass of orange juice, wiped the corners of her sensuous mouth with the well starched white napkin and picked up her sports bag from the corner of the room.

'Bye darling,' she called over her shoulder went through the door and Sir Humphrey grunted yet again behind his newspaper as he heard the front door close solidly behind her.

Ginger sat up as he saw her leave and watched as she skipped down the four stone steps and remotely operate the central locking on one of those dinky little Off Road' vehicles which would never be driven off road in its entire life. He started the Astra's engine and pulled round into Eaton Place keeping a respectable distance behind the White RAV 4'. As he followed she turned into Ebury Street, along Pimlico Road and across Sloane Street into Royal Hospital Road to join the Embankment by the Chelsea Physic Garden. The traffic was heavier along the Embankment and Ginger just saw her double back along Cheyne Walk just before the Albert Bridge. She stopped outside an exclusive fitness club jumped out nimbly, fed a parking meter with coins and disappeared inside. Ginger parked a couple of spaces back, fed his meter and settled down for another wait. He had learnt patience during his time in the army. He could sit quite still for hours on end without getting in the least bored.

It was just over an hour later when Samantha reappeared but not in the smart expensive looking white jogging suit. This time she was wearing a pale blue pleated skirt and a white polo necked, figure hugging sweater. She must keep a change of clothes at the club. Her marvellous auburn hair was now tied up into a pony tail with a pale blue chiffon scarf which was an exact match for the skirt. He saw the two orange lights flick on and off twice as she walked towards the four wheel drive and got in throwing her sports bag into the back. She pulled out into the busy early morning traffic and was soon indicating to turn left into Oakley Street. Ginger was having a job keeping her in sight. She had found a gap in the traffic but he had not been so fortunate and was now at least four cars behind her. He pulled out slightly just in time to see her turning right into the Kings

Road. Eventually, by means of some tricky driving, he was now only two cars behind her as she drove quickly and expertly in the heavy traffic. Once again he spotted, just in time, that she was indicating to turn left just before the Kings Walk Shopping Mall. Once again he was lucky to find a space just across the road from where Samantha had parked. He settled down for a longer wait this time. She had walked into an exclusive ladies hairdressers.

Two hours later he could see why she had been so long. She looked amazing. The pony tail had gone and her hair was now much shorter and styled immaculately. She didn't go back to her car and Ginger had to move a bit smartly to put more coins in the meter and catch up with her as she moved out into a crowded Kings Road. She crossed over the road opposite the shopping mall and carried on until she came to a coffee bar. It wasn't the sort of coffee bar that Ginger was used to but as he was dressed in his dark business suit he followed her inside. She joined two other women in a booth by the window and he slipped into the next one along sitting with his back to her. He ordered an espresso and was astounded by the figure on the little pink slip which accompanied it. He had no difficulty hearing what was being said in the next booth. The ladies were in good form and their voices would have been registering high on a decibel meter had there been one. He wondered how he was going to make his coffee last as they chattered on about their many mutual friends. There must have been a lot of ears burning around the capital that morning. Three quarters of an hour later he had reluctantly ordered another very expensive coffee. The ladies were on their third. However, the wait was worthwhile. He was, at last, starting to hear something interesting. Lady Samantha was telling them with great enthusiasm about her having been asked to present prizes at somewhere called Queensbridge which, as the conversation progressed, turned out to be her old school. Apparently she and Sir Humphrey were going to travel down to the school, which was situated somewhere near Chippenham in Wiltshire, late the following afternoon. The prize giving would be followed by the school's Annual Ball and it was going to be fabulous she was babbling on. On and on about the terribly expensive new dress she had bought, the shoes, the diamond necklace and ear rings. On and on. Ginger was almost asleep when they finally started their protracted goodbyes which were accompanied by much hugging and kissing on both cheeks, each kiss missing by miles. When they finally tore themselves away from each other he could see Samantha making her way back towards the car and stood up to follow her. He was glad to be on his feet again and out of the claustrophobic atmosphere of the cafe. He followed her back to Eaton Place and settled down for another long wait. As he sat he started thinking about Samantha's trip to Wiltshire. The more he thought about it the more he thought that, if Charlie was really serious about abducting her, that they would probably never ever get a better opportunity. It would be far easier down in the country than attempting something in the city. The school would almost certainly stand in its own grounds. The ballroom would be hot. People would drift out into the open air with their drinks. It would be dark. Yes the more he thought about it the more he liked the idea. He took out his mobile phone and hesitated before dialling Charlie's number. It wasn't exactly an emergency he thought but it was a golden opportunity and he was sure that Charlie would appreciate it. He would just have to risk her being within earshot of Norman when her phone rang.

CHAPTER EIGHTEEN

Back at the farm Charlie had just nipped upstairs to get something from her handbag. As she bent to pick up the bag from the side of the bed the phone rang inside it. She jumped back startled by the sudden sound then recovered and quickly delved in to stop the infernal thing beeping. She held it to ear hoping that the sound hadn't travelled downstairs. She needn't have worried. The thick walls and doors of the old house didn't allow much sound to penetrate them.

'Ginger?' It had to be Ginger. He was the only one who knew the number.

'What the hell are you playing at? We agreed that you would only ring in an emergency. What's happened?'

'Sorry hen. Is Norman there?'

'No, as it happens, but that's not the bloody point. What is so important that you have to ring me here?'

'Look, if it's difficult to talk at the moment, go somewhere where you can and call me back. You've got the number.'

'OK,' she said angrily - ,just give me half an hour,' and with that she snapped the phone shut and replaced it her bag. Just then she heard Norman coming up the stairs.

'Who are you talking to,' he enquired as he entered the bedroom.

'Myself. I'm afraid it's a bad habit of mine. They say it's the first sign that one is going out of one's mind. Did you want something?'

'No, I was just coming up to the bathroom. Are you OK? You look a little distracted.'

'I'm fine,' she replied a little too quickly,

'I just came up to get some money,' she lied, 'we need some milk. I'm just going to slip down to the village. I shan't be long.' And with that she ran lightly down the stairs and out to the car.

Sitting outside the village store she took the mobile out of her bag and dialled Ginger's number.

'Robson!' the gruff Scottish voice answered.

'It's me, Charlie. What the hell is the matter Ginger?'

'Calm down lassie. I have just found out something which I thought you ought to know about today. Saturday will be too late. It appears that your friend Samantha is going to be out of town tomorrow and Saturday. Apparently she is giving out prizes at her old school tomorrow evening. A place called Queensbridge, somewhere near Chippenham.'

'Yes, yes, I know where Queensbridge is. It happens to be one of my old schools.' She sounded impatient.

'Well in view of our conversation yesterday I thought that we ought to meet up somewhere. Preferably somewhere near Chippenham if you can make it. I don't trust these bloody mobile things. Too many people listening in for my liking.'

'As it happens Norman and I are only about an hour's drive from there. How soon can you be there? We could meet up at Leigh Delamere Services on the M4. We can get on the motorway at Junction 17 if we drive across through Malmesbury. This means I will have to tell Norman sooner than I had intended but if you insist that it is urgent then so be it.'

'Right lassie, I can be there by two thirty, three at the latest I'll see you there,' and the phone went dead. Not one to waste words our Ginger she thought.

She dashed into the store and picked up a carton of milk and drove back to the farm. As she entered the kitchen the smell of bacon and eggs met her. Norman had started preparing lunch.

'Hi!' she called out as she popped the milk in the fridge and went over to the sink to fill the kettle. When they were sat down at the huge square table in the centre of the kitchen well into their lunch she said tentatively,

'Norman I have something to tell you. Please don't be angry. I'm afraid I have been behind your back and have discussed an idea I've had with Ginger.'

Norman swallowed a mouthful of food and started to speak. Charlie held up her hand and said,

'Please Norman, let me finish, please. The explosive idea was fine but the authorities are obviously playing silly beggars, not acknowledging our claims. They could go on for ever with that caper. Well, as I said, I have had another idea. It came to me when we were watching that chat show in the hotel in Cirencester. Samantha, you remember. Wife of Sir Humphrey Simpkins, at the Ministry of Transport. I thought why not go right to the top. Why not abduct his wife and hold her until someone takes notice of our demands.'

'Bloody hell Charlie,' Norman sounded appalled.

'I thought I was the one with all the crazy ideas. Are you seriously suggesting that we get involved in abduction. My God, if we were to get caught they would bang us up and throw away the key, if only to discourage any other group or individual trying the same thing. I don't like it. What does Ginger say about it? Does he think that we can get away with it?'

Charlie was beginning to have doubts now and said nervously,

'You can ask him yourself. I've arranged for us to meet him this afternoon on the M4. I'm afraid that will probably mean having to put tonight's plan on hold until we have spoken with him.'

'Well, it seems that you have everything organised", Norman said a little sharply.

'There is someone else I must ring,' she said as she too the tiny mobile phone from her handbag.

Norman looked at the phone,

'My word, we have been busy.'

'Please don't be angry Norman, this next phone call is going to be difficult enough. I'm going to phone mummy. All the time I was away at college she used to send me all the newsletters and school magazines from Queensbridge. I am just hoping that (a), she will speak to me and (b), that the school is still sending stuff to the house.'

She sat down in the living room and dialled a number. Norman had never seen her look so agitated since he had met her. Eventually the phone was answered.

'Hello mummy, it's me, Charlie. No mummy please don't hang up. Yes I know. I'm so sorry . . . I understand how hurt you must have been. I behaved terribly when daddy died. I rang to ask if I could come and see you this afternoon. I can't apologise properly over the phone. Please mummy. Jeremy won't be there will he? I don't think that I could face him yet. Thanks mummy. I'll see you about one thirty if that's alright. Bye.'

She looked quite pale as she broke the connection and there was the faintest film of perspiration on her brow. Norman took her in his arms and hugged her tightly.

'That really took some doing didn't it love.'

She didn't answer but just cradled her head on his shoulder for quite some time. After a while he held her at arms-length and asked,

'Do you want me to come with you?'

'You can drive me down there but I must talk to mummy alone. You don't mind do you? It will take the best part of an hour to drive down to Warminster. I should be able to spend an hour or so there before we have to leave to meet Ginger. You wouldn't believe the number of times that I have thought of making that phone call and then chickened out. I know that it won't be easy meeting face to face but I already feel as though a great weight has been lifted.'

They set off within minutes and had a good run down to her mother's. It was a large mock Georgian house which stood well back from the road beyond an immaculate garden. Norman stopped the car just beyond the driveway and Charlie got out. When she was only halfway to the front door it opened and her mother stood there with her arms outstretched. Charlie ran the rest of the way up the drive and threw herself towards her mother and they stood there holding each other, crying uncontrollably. Norman felt rather uncomfortable. He felt as though he was intruding. After what seemed ages the two women parted slowly and her mother asked Charlie,

'Who is you friend? Aren't you going to ask him in?'

Not this time mummy,' she said inferring that there would be other visits and that she would introduce him then.

'Norman understands that WE have a lot of catching up to do.'

With that they disappeared into the house and Norman settled down with the paperback which he had brought along to pass the time. It was well over an hour when the front door opened again and he glanced sideways to see Charlie hugging her mother and then making her way back to the car. He was glad that the two of them had obviously made up. Life's too short for that sort of thing. He knew only too well. He and Jenny hadn't often quarrelled but since the accident he regarded every second that they had spent at odds with each other as a complete waste of time.

In the event Charlie had not had to ask about the stuff from Queensbridge and she was very relieved about that. Had she gone about it in the wrong way she could have ruined everything. As it happened, when her mother had brought in the tea tray she had given her a bundle of magazines and newsletters. I have been saving these for you darling she had said, and Charlie had inwardly said a big thank you God.

As they drove round the corner she waved through the window and when they were about a hundred yards down the main road she was already sifting through the pile.

'Bingo,' she shouted after a couple of minutes, holding up an invitation to the Annual Prize Giving and Ball at Queensbridge.

'This could prove to be crucial to my plan,' she said triumphantly.

'Let's go and meet Ginger! ! !'

CHAPTER NINETEEN

Ginger was on his second cup of coffee when he saw Charlie and Norman come into the cafeteria. He waved them over and Charlie went to sit next to him whilst Norman picked up a pot of tea for two.

'Sorry we are so late,' she said slipping off her lightweight jacket,

'I have been to see my mother. It was the first time we have spoken since my father died. We have made up now I'm pleased to say but I still feel a little bit ashamed because there was an ulterior motive for my visit. She showed Ginger the invitation to the prize giving. This might prove invaluable if we decide to go ahead with our plan tomorrow night.'

When they were all seated Ginger started to tell them both in detail about the conversation he had overheard in the coffee bar in the Kings Road.

'So do you think we could pull it off?' asked Norman sounding sceptical.

'Bear in mind that, if they are attending the function together, the Police Inspector is certain to be with them.'

'Yes,' Charlie broke in,

'But what you must remember is that she has a reputation for shaking off her escort much to her husband's chagrin. The forecast for tomorrow is hot and humid so there will probably be as many people outside as inside once the ball starts. The school hall where the dance will be held has several double glass doors down the side which open onto the lawns leading to the playing fields. No doubt there will be more than one or two couples sneaking off into the undergrowth during the evening. There will be groups standing around, drinks in hand, seeking some relief from the sweltering heat of the dance floor.'

Ginger produced an A5 sketch pad from his hold-all and passed it to Charlie.

'Do you think you could draw a fairly accurate plan of the layout of the place showing the hall in relation to the grounds and if possible the roads leading to and from the school?'

'It has been several years but, yes, I think that I could give you a pretty detailed plan,' and with that she picked up the fibre tip pen which Ginger passed across the table.

While Charlie set about her sketch plan the other two discussed the logistics of a possible abduction.

' I notice that the invitation is for Miss Forbes-Smythe and guest,' said Ginger,

'So you are the obvious choice for the role of guest. That sort of thing isn't my scene. I suggest that you hire yourself an evening suit. I presume it is black tie. You and Charlie will use your car and I'll take the van.'

Norman noticed the subtle change from "you could use" to "you will use". Ginger was already presuming that the operation was on and he decided to go along with that presumption for the time being. He could make his mind up later when he was convinced whether or not the whole thing was feasible.

Ginger was carrying on,

'It might be a good idea if we were to paint out the ' Landscape Gardener' legend on the van. That was OK for driving up and down the motorways but the van may have to be parked up for quite a few hours and the more anonymous it looks the better. Look we can't stay here for ever and it's not the place to do the planning for this kind of thing.'

'You're right,' said Norman,

'Why don't we go back to the farm and make ourselves comfortable. I have a feeling that we will be burning the midnight oil tonight.'

Charlie who had been working on the sketch plan was also listening to every word that was being said. She nodded in agreement and suggested that they drive down to Chippenham which was only about fifteen minute's drive from where they were sitting.

'A quick look around the surrounding lanes would just refresh my memory. I can recall the layout of the school quite well but the local geography is a bit hazy.'

'Agreed,' said Ginger,

'I'll follow in my car.'

Two hours later they were sat around the large table in the kitchen eating a hastily prepared tea. When they had finished the meal they cleared the table and Charlie began to transfer her quick

A5 sketch onto a much larger piece of paper. Meanwhile Norman took Ginger down to the barn where the van was parked. As they went into the building in the fading light Norman noted with amusement the puzzled look on Ginger's face. There wasn't a vehicle to be seen. In the poor light the front row of bales blended with the ones behind. Norman led the way to where the van and the car were hidden.

'Ingenious,' Ginger said rather sarcastically,

'You always were a clever sod. All the same it's a bloody good idea and having seen this, another idea springs to mind. If the lady in question is to be our guest for any length of time this might be a far better place to keep her rather than the farm house. We could purchase a large two berth tent and set it up in here behind the bales away from prying eyes. We could install a chemical toilet in one section and put one of the very comfortable camp beds, which are available these days, in the other. Let's get back to the house and compile a comprehensive list of all the things we will need starting with a large aerosol can of dark green paint for the van.'

It was turned midnight by the time they had

completed their list and had studied Charlie's exceptionally detailed plan of the school and surrounding area. They turned in and Norman set his alarm for seven the following morning.

After breakfast on the Friday morning, in order to save time, Charlie had dialled the "Talking Pages" service and had obtained a list of camping and outdoor pursuit outlets. The nearest and, the one which sounded like the best of these, turned out to be only about twenty minute's drive from the farm. It was a large, high class store which catered for every type of outdoor pursuit and was situated, of all places, just inside the entrance to a caravan holiday park.

When they had enquired at the village store they had been told to go to the main road and turn north towards Cirencester and then follow the brown road signs for a place called Hoburne Cotswold which was apparently in the Cotswold Water Parks.

They had all driven up in the van which unfortunately still bore the lettering proclaiming J. Simpson & Son, Landscape Gardeners. They had decided to re-spray the van panels as soon as they returned to the farm. The store was extremely well stocked and they were able to purchase every single item on their list and the van was almost full as they drove out through the main gate of the park. They made a quick trip up to Cirencester, found a car accessory shop on the outskirts of the town and bought two large spray tins of dark green cellulose paint.

During the afternoon, while Ginger was doing an expert job of spraying the van panels, Charlie and Norman were busy erecting a luxury four berth tent on a thick bed of hay covered with a heavy duty ground sheet. The tent was behind the screen of bales well over to the right hand side of the barn so as to allow room for the cars and the van to be hidden as well. It was one of the modern tents in which people camped in comparative luxury for weeks on end. It consisted of three main compartments. Two bedrooms each with zip fastened covers which ensured complete privacy and a third area at the front which could be used as a kitchen and living space during the daytime. Outside the tent on the wall of the barn were three large metal rings. These must have been used at some time for tethering animals and were very sturdy.

Norman had cut a neat circular hole in the side of the tent nearest the wall and had passed through it one end of a coil of blue nylon rope and he tied it very securely to one of the rings. On the other end of the rope which was coiled up neatly on the floor of one of the "bedrooms" was a broad leather belt of the sort used by mountaineers. The only difference was that this belt was also equipped with a large brass padlock. In the same room was a comfortable camp bed, a canvas chair and a white plastic topped folding table. In the other room was a chemical toilet together with a folding canvas sink on an aluminium stand. There were also two large red plastic buckets which were already filled with water.

When Ginger was satisfied with his paint job he came round to inspect the "accommodation". He walked slowly round in silence and after ten minutes or so he nodded his approval.

'That looks fine. I don't think that we have forgotten anything. I think that we should all go indoors now and have an hours rest. We can't plan anything too rigid for tonight. We will just have to play it by ear depending on her Ladyship's behaviour. The only thing that we can say for certain is that I will drive the van and if the worst comes to the worst I will handle any rough stuff which may be necessary. You two will clear off in the car and will not, repeat not get involved under any circumstances. Don't worry about me, I can take care of myself. I could exist for weeks living rough on Salisbury Plain. I've done it several times before.'

It was like old times, Norman thought. Sergeant Robson was taking control as he had always done. Norman was quite happy with the situation and he settled back in one of the large armchairs and shut his eyes.

CHAPTER TWENTY

Back at West Midlands Police Headquarters Superintendent Laidlow was sitting at his desk staring at one of the yellow
"F O R B O R"
posters. He looked across at Newman who was sat in silence watching his boss intently.

'It has got me puzzled Sergeant and I don't like being puzzled. I find it very strange that we haven't heard anything further from these people. These so called "Ecco Warriors" are usually full of themselves. Constantly shouting the odds about their cause. This lot are either being very crafty, hoping that we will eventually reveal their demands to the media, or they are amateurs who don't know what the bloody hell to do next because we haven't given them the publicity they expected. I don't like it. We have no leads to speak of. All we know is that the person who may have bought the materials to produce these posters is an attractive blonde who may or may not work for a landscape gardener. Did you manage to get hold of the tapes from Traffic which were recorded immediately before the two towers went down?'

'Yes Sir. I have got them set up on the video if you would like to see them.'

'OK let's have a look at them, although I must admit I don't hold out much hope that they will reveal anything useful.'

Newman started the first tape running. He had set up the tapes so that they ran for half an hour before each of the respective towers went down. They sat and watched the endless procession of traffic going away from them north up the M5. Newman, despite the fact that he was on the accelerated promotion programme was not above doing some good old fashioned police plodding and he had already gone through the tapes several times. He was intrigued to see if his superior would spot the interesting coincidence on the first two tapes which he was going to run. The third tape which, was to be his *piece de resistance*, he had selected from several tapes from further down the motorway which he had decided to look at on a mere hunch. Not the modern scientific method of investigation, but then perhaps something was rubbing off from Bill Laidlow. The younger man had, in the short time he had known him, developed a great respect for his boss.

Superintendent Laidlow was puffing away contentedly at his ancient pipe and was showing no reaction whatsoever. In fact Newman wasn't entirely sure that he was still awake. He need not have been concerned. Laidlow was concentrating his full attention on the tapes. After half an hour the screen suddenly went dead and Newman reached across to change the tape. The following half hour followed exactly the same pattern and as the second tape finished Laidlow was already standing up.

'Could you just bear with me for a little longer Sir?'

Newman sounded anxious and Laidlow reluctantly sat down again.

'This third tape was amongst several I looked through on a hunch of mine.'

Laidlow smiled to himself at the word hunch. Perhaps the lad was learning something after all he thought.

'It's from the Strensham service area,' Newman continued, ' And was recorded about half an hour after the second tower went down. I noticed that on the first two tapes that there was, in both cases, a Motorway Maintenance van in the vicinity as the towers went down. The first instance was as the first tower went down the van was proceeding south away from the scene. Just before the second one went down the van was travelling south on the opposite carriageway. Nothing unusual about that you might say but on the third tape which I am about to show you a similar Ford Transit van entered the car park at Strensham. A young attractive blonde jumped out obviously desperate to visit the ladies toilets. Two minutes later she got back into the van and drove over to the furthest point on the car park. Having parked she got out, despite the heavy rain, ran round to the back and climbed in. The van then stayed there for quite some time. I must admit that it was the girl that got my attention in the first place but then her odd behaviour intrigued me and I took the tape together with the two we have just watched to a chum of mine in the computer centre. He can work wonders with video tapes and he put mine up on his screen and zoomed into the van and greatly enhanced the image. The first thing that struck me was the lettering on the side of the van. It read,

"J. Simpson & Son, Landscape Gardeners"

Then as the van pulled away to the far end of the car park we had a good view of the registration number which we noted. Then we went back to the first tapes to have a look at the maintenance van and, much to our dismay, the registration number was the same and yet the wording "Motorway Maintenance" was clearly visible on the side.'

'Bloody well done lad. We'll make a copper of you yet,' said Laidlow with genuine admiration for the younger man's perseverance.

'I presume that you have checked the number with Swansea.'

'Yes Sir, and that threw up another anomaly. The vehicle is registered to Warwickshire County Council and is indeed a Motorway Maintenance van, but on the day in question that particular van was in the council workshops having a service prior to taking it's MOT test.'

'Now that is interesting Sergeant. That means that there are either two or possibly three vans bearing the same registration number. Probably two. The van in which we are interested probably has changeable side panels. Make sure that every Traffic division in the country has that number and I want to be informed the minute it is spotted. Also I would like you to put out a top security alert for any mention of the acronym FORBOR. If this name crops up anywhere I must be informed at once, day or night. Please emphasise that under no circumstances what so ever should any local action be taken. Once again, well done Martin.'

Newman beamed. It was the first time the "Super" had ever called him by his first name.

* * * * *

At the very same time that Laidlow and Newman were viewing the tapes and discussing the strange matter of the registration number of the van, Ginger, as if by some sort of telepathy, decided that it would be wise to change to one of the other sets of number plates which they had in reserve. The van had been using the same set ever since leaving London the previous weekend. No point in taking unnecessary chances especially as the van would probably be parked in the same place for quite a long time that evening.

As he knelt on the earth floor of the barn changing the number plates Charlie came in with a large mug of steaming hot tea. She squatted on her haunches watching Ginger work and started tentatively,

'Do you think that we can pull it off Ginger?'

'We can do anything if we put our minds to it and if we really want to succeed. You DO want us to succeed don't you, because if either you or Norman is having second thoughts just say so now. It's no use getting cold feet on the night. That could land the lot of us in the slammer. Just you go back to the house now and talk to Norman. I want both of you to be absolutely sure that you want to go through with this. Once we have started there will be no turning back.'

Charlie stood up, pushed her hands deep into the pockets of her jeans and headed slowly for the door. Of course Ginger had seen this sort of reaction many times before. Most of the men with whom he had gone into action had had a bout of the shakes a few hours before the start, but ninety nine out a hundred of them were fine once things got going and the adrenaline started to flow. He had been in action with Norman and knew that he could rely on him once his mind was made up but Charlie was an unknown factor.

Norman was staring out of the window as Charlie walked in and she said,

'Well are we raring to go tonight?'

Norman turned round and forced a smile. In fact he had been stood there in the same position for about ten minutes debating with himself the very same question.

'I certainly am,' he said hoping to detect something in her voice or her expression which would indicate her own feelings on the forthcoming events,

'Yes I think it's a bloody great idea,' he continued,

'Far less risky than placing explosives on motorways. If we can get her ladyship back here to the farm without being spotted I don't think that the authorities will have a clue where to start looking.'

Charlie didn't know whether to be reassured or be more worried. She had a funny feeling that Norman was putting on an act, but she couldn't be sure and so she decided to go along with the enthusiastic mood.

Back in the barn Ginger was busy with the van. He was carefully checking everything. Fuel and oil levels. tyre pressures, battery connections. He had learned long ago from bitter experience that, no matter how well the men are trained, no matter how many times you have gone over the plans, it is so often the smallest, most stupid mechanical fault that can screw up the whole operation. He was determined to eliminate as many risks as possible before they set off that extraordinary evening.

CHAPTER TWENTY ONE

Norman was still struggling with his bow tie as Charlie came into the bedroom. She had insisted on getting ready in one of the other bedrooms. She had said that she wanted to surprise him and by God she had.

'You look bloody marvellous,' said Norman as he stood with his mouth open taking in the beautiful vision before him. Charlie smiled to herself. She hadn't expected to have such a devastating effect on him. He had forgotten the tangled mess around his collar and was just staring at her.

She DID look bloody marvellous. Her make up had been meticulously applied but not over stated. There was a hint of green eye shadow which picked up the colour of her dress. Her pale pink lipstick accentuated her lovely sensuous mouth and her flawless skin had only the slightest covering of a good quality powder. The new green dress, which she had bought on her trip into Swindon, fitted her perfectly and Norman could see the outline of her well-shaped breasts beneath the fine material. The most striking feature of the dress however was the skirt. It was quite short and hung from a low waist line in a flair of very fine pleats. As he watched she did a little twirl and the skirt spun out to reveal a glimpse of the tiny matching lycra briefs underneath, together with the lacy tops of her glossy stockings.

'Well?' she said, 'Will I do?'

Norman was speechless. All he wanted to do was to take her in his arms and kiss those lovely pink lips but Charlie put her hands on his shoulders and held him at arms-length.

'Now, let's have a look at this tie. You're making a real mess of it. By the way, how clever of you to choose a green bow tie. Have you been peeking in my shopping?'

Norman had no idea why he had picked the tie. He had selected and tried on the evening suit and the tie had just caught his eye. It was quite a dark green so not too flashy and he thought that it would make a change from the boring old black which he would normally have chosen. He had put that down to the effect Charlie was having on him but he had no idea about the dress until a couple of minutes ago.

When they went down stairs Ginger greeted them with an exaggerated intake of breath.

'My, what a handsome couple. You'll be the Belle of the Ball lassie, and you don't scrub up too badly either young Nosey,' he said with a broad grin on his face.

Ginger, for his part, was dressed in complete contrast to the young couple. He was wearing a dark polo neck sweater, black jeans and dark coloured trainers. Norman had seen him dressed like this on many occasions and knew that, later in the evening, he would complete the outfit with a black balaclava helmet to conceal his red hair.

'Right you two . . . the moment of truth. One last chance to make sure that you want to go through with this. You could just go down there and have a wonderful evening. It's "make your mind up" time.'

They answered, almost in unison, declaring that they both wanted to go ahead with the abduction of Lady Samantha Simpkins.

'OK,' said Ginger,

'If you are both quite sure then it's time we were making a move. You don't want to make yourselves too conspicuous by arriving late and pushing your way along a row of seats when the proceedings have got under way,' and with that they went out to the vehicles. Charlie and Norman got into the car and Ginger climbed up into the Transit van. It was a warm, pleasant evening as they drove out of the farmyard and made their way to the main road south towards Swindon. They would arrive at Queensbridge in about three quarters of an hour barring hold ups, (for which they had allowed another fifteen minutes).

Norman and Charlie pulled into the gravelled drive of the school with plenty of time to spare and parked under the branches of a large cedar tree. Norman had parked well back down the drive, firstly to be near the gates if they needed to make a quick exit and secondly, he wasn't too keen on parking his modest family saloon any closer to the main buildings amongst the range of cars which included Rolls, Bentleys, Merc's and BMW's.

Before they went into the school for the Prize Giving ceremony, Norman walked back down the drive and out through the gates to check where Ginger had parked. He couldn't see him at first and was just about to start walking in the other direction when he saw the van's headlights flick quickly on and off. Ginger had pulled the van well back into the hedgerow on the opposite side of the road from the wall which surrounded the grounds of Queensbridge. From where he sat he could see the main gates but, as Norman had found out, he could not be seen clearly himself.

'You and Charlie had better get inside now. We can't do anything until the dance is well underway. I'll contact you when you come out into the grounds and don't panic, I'll be discreet,' he said seeing the worried look which had briefly crossed Norman's face.

The hall was a hub-hub of chatter as they took their seats. Charlie looked around her but could see no one that she recognised. Hardly surprising, she thought, when one considered just how many girls had passed through these hallowed corridors over the years. She could well be the only girl from her year. Of course the one Old Girl whom she would be certain to recognise would be Samantha. Beautiful, elegant Samantha.

Norman was feeling less uncomfortable as the lights went down and the school orchestra struck up with the introduction to the School Song. He sat there cringing and wondered how every school orchestra in the world managed to sound exactly the same as this one. Totally excruciating! However when the choir started singing, just before the heavy velvet curtains swished back, the hairs on the back of his neck stood on end. He had never heard anything so amazing. As the curtains parted they revealed the girls aged from about eleven or twelve to seventeen or eighteen all immaculately turned out in the school uniform of white blouse worn with the school tie of gold and maroon stripes and pleated maroon skirt. The sound of their voices rose as the muffling effect of the curtains was removed.

Norman sat there transfixed and when they had finished he clapped enthusiastically and almost stood up but checked himself just in time. Charlie turned and smiled at him. She hadn't expected a reaction like that. Norman was full of surprises. She had expected that he would sit there fidgeting, bored out of his mind.

The stage cleared of girls to reveal two rows of gold coloured chairs which were occupied by mistresses and a couple of masters of the school. In the centre of the front row sat the headmistress who was flanked on the one side by Sir Humphrey Simpkins and on the other by Lady Samantha. Just out of sight standing behind the curtain stood Detective Inspector Barnes and his eyes were darting everywhere. His was the unenviable job of trying to protect Sir Humphrey and Lady Samantha, the latter causing him to grow old long before his time. He had already asked twice for a transfer but had been turned down. He lived in constant dread of something happening to her, not because he was unduly worried for her well being, but the thought of loosing the pension for which he had worked so hard appalled him.

Charlie heard the little gasp which came from Norman's lips when he first saw Samantha. Mind you she had to admit, she did look stunning. The mass of auburn hair was taken up on top of her head revealing a neck which resembled a slim marble pillar. The creamy white neck was further enhanced by a diamond necklace which, Norman estimated, must have cost well into five figures. Her pale turquoise dress set off her spectacular colouring. The plunging neckline emphasised her full breasts and the clever styling nipped in at her slim waist and sat comfortably over her generous hips, the hem of the skirt barely touching her knees as she sat with her legs crossed elegantly.

The headmistress was on her feet now droning on and on about the many achievements of the previous year and although Norman was stifling a yawn his gaze was flitting between Samantha's legs and her wonderful cleavage. He was jolted from his reverie by a muted ripple of applause as the elderly lady finally sat down.

Then Samantha was on her feet and he was aware of an acute change of mood. The girls and parents were suddenly sitting more upright in their seats. Samantha was launching into a speech which was grabbing everybody's attention. No yawns now. No shifting from cheek to cheek on the bum deadening chairs. She had their full attention. She was relating to the girls. She was speaking their language and as she sat down the girls and their families were on their feet clapping and cheering. Even the headmistress, who had looked decidedly uneasy at the start of the speech, was up on her feet clapping with the rest of them. It was as if a breath of fresh air had swept through the old building.

Then the actual prize giving started and Norman noticed how Samantha had a little chat with each of the recipients. Not the usual cool hand shake and curt "Well Done" but a genuine interest in each of the girls' achievements. He found himself warming to this woman who, only a couple of weeks ago, as he had watched that morning chat show, had considered to be something of an "air head". He had obviously been quite wrong in his first appraisal.

CHAPTER TWENTY TWO

When the applause had died down the head girl entered from stage left with a huge bouquet of flowers which she presented to Samantha with an immaculate little curtsy. As she retreated shyly to the side of the stage the Chairman of Governors got to his feet and invited the audience to take a short tour of the school while the room was being cleared and prepared for the dance. He was most insistent that they should not miss the schools latest acquisition . . . a prestigious new science block. Slowly, parents and girls set off dutifully in small groups on their tour of inspection. Norman and Charlie tagged on behind a small group who were so busy chatting that they didn't even notice them. This suited them and as they walked down the corridors of the old school they maintained an air of complete anonymity.

Meanwhile, out in the grounds, Ginger, who had now donned his black balaclava, was quietly surveying the grounds. He moved about silently in the shadows taking time to get his bearings. He rounded a corner to be confronted by an incongruous structure of tinted glass, stainless steel and concrete. It was, of course, the new science block. Ginger, who was by no means an expert in architecture, was appalled by this monstrosity that had been stuck carelessly onto the east wall of the elegant old building which had been designed and built two centuries before.

He continued around the grounds looking for alternative exits but it looked as though the only feasible way out was down the drive, especially if one of the party was going to be reluctant to leave. He decided to risk bringing the van into the grounds and parked it in a space under the same cedar tree as Norman's car. He didn't like the idea much but the chances of getting Samantha all the way down the drive unnoticed were pretty slim.

Back inside the hall the members of the seven piece orchestra were taking their places on the stage. No noisy, thumping disco for Queensbridge. Here, they insisted on maintaining certain standards, which in a changing world, was very reassuring to parents when they were choosing a school for their daughters. Ten minutes later the Chairman of Governors who was also acting as Master of Ceremonies was on stage inviting Sir Humphrey and Lady Samantha to lead off the first dance and get the proceedings underway.

The floor was filling quickly with couples and Norman held his hand out to Charlie and they joined the throng. Ginger had been right . . . they could have had a bloody good night out under other circumstances. It had been a long, long time since Norman had held a girl close to him on a dance floor and he was really enjoying it. It was Charlie who broke the spell,

'We will have to think of a way of getting Samantha out into the grounds soon.'

Reluctantly, they left the floor and went over to the long table which was serving as a bar and ran the length of the hall. As they reached the table Samantha arrived and stood right next to Charlie. She had a very good looking young man on her arm and there was no sign of Sir Humphrey.

As they turned to leave the bar, Charlie backed into Samantha, as if by accident. The two women turned to face each other and it looked, for a moment, as though Samantha was going to rebuke her for being so clumsy. But then her face creased into that famous smile as she recognised Charlie.

'Charlotte darling,' she said making, but just failing to kiss her on both cheeks in that affected way that her type do.

'It is Charlotte isn't it? How lovely to see you. Let's go outside and chat, it's so dammed hot in here,' and turning to the young man she said,

'Be a love Tarquin and take these drinks outside,' she pushed two glasses of champagne into his hands and he turned obediently to do her bidding.

Tarquin, thought Norman, dead right, he looks a right bloody Tarquin

'He's a bit of a dream but he has more money than sense and I just couldn't resist that fantastic body. I suspect that I will give him a good screwing before the night is over,' she said, quite matter of casually.

They moved into the relative cool of the balmy evening outside and Norman was amazed just how easy it had been made for them. Inspector Barnes followed them at a discreet distance but the fact wasn't lost on Norman and his mind was already working on a way to get rid of him.

Samantha launched into a series of questions enquiring what Charlie had been doing since leaving the school.

'She could have played netball for England had she put her mind to it,' she said turning to Norman and without waiting for a reply or even a nod she was off again. They were standing with their backs to a sort of semi-circle formed by a dense grove of Rhododendrons when Norman suddenly felt a light tap on the shoulder. He somehow fought the urge to jump and turned his head slightly and signalled to Ginger with a nod of his head that the Inspector was only a few feet away just out of his line of vision.

'I'll try to get rid of him and then we must be

ready to move' Ginger whispered. Neither Charlie nor Samantha had seen or heard any of this. They were too engrossed with each other.

'Try to get her a bit further down the drive towards the tree where you parked your car if you can manage it. The van is there also,' and with that he was gone as silently as he had appeared.

Ginger momentarily removed his balaclava when he spotted a young girl, probably a firstt year, hurrying towards the ball room. He walked quickly alongside her and said, with a hint of urgency,

'I wonder if you could give a message to that gentleman over there,' indicating the Detective Inspector,

'Could you tell him, please, that Sir Humphrey Simpkins needs to speak to him. It is very urgent.'

The little girl turned immediately and started quickly towards the policeman, quite delighted to have been chosen for this important chore. Ginger stood back in the shadows and watched as Barnes glanced quickly in the direction of Samantha, shrugged his shoulders and moved off quickly towards the school hall to find Sir

Humphrey. He was probably going to be told to round up Lady Samantha and take her to the car. Sir Humphrey didn't like these functions and Barnes knew from experience that he would be champing at the bit, anxious to return to their hotel before her Ladyship committed any serious indiscretion.

As soon as the Inspector disappeared into the building Ginger headed back to where he had left Norman and the others and noted with satisfaction that the little group was moving almost imperceptibly towards the van.

It was Norman who was speaking now and he was waving his arms about. God knows what he's on about thought Ginger but, whatever it is, it's working just fine. He disappeared into the bushes again and followed the group's progress slowly down the drive. They were now about twenty yards from the van and had stopped. They looked as though they were about to turn and start back towards the hall and Ginger decided that it was now or never. There was hardly anyone about this far from the hall and he darted out from the undergrowth, grabbed Samantha from behind placing his hand over her mouth to stifle any attempt at a scream. Norman and Charlie looked genuinely startled and the young man who had carried the drinks out proved to be pretty quick on his feet. He shot after Ginger and grabbed him.

'I say, what's going on,' he said in his plummy voice.

Ginger still holding one hand over Samantha's mouth straightened the fingers of his free hand and jabbed into Tarquin's throat and he immediately collapsed in a heap. Ginger rolled him over with his foot until he was out of sight under a large Azalea bush. He dragged the girl roughly towards the van followed closely by Norman and Charlie who were shouting abuse at him and demanding that he release her at once. They were putting on a good act thought Ginger. He bundled her into the back of the Transit. He had previously lifted the false floor to reveal the mattress so she had a soft landing but by the time she had recovered enough to turn round the van door was already being slammed in her face. She hadn't seen anything, let alone his face. He had been behind her the entire time.

Ginger started the van and drove slowly down the drive and through the gates. He knew from experience that nothing draws more attention than a quickly accelerating vehicle. Norman and Charlie had a quick look around before climbing into the car and following Ginger. They had been extraordinarily lucky. The party was in full swing in and it seemed that everyone was facing towards the bright lights of the building deep in their respective conversations.

About five minutes later Inspector Barnes came striding out from one of the French windows. He had finally found Sir Humphrey only to be told that he had not been sent for.

'You had better get yourself outside Inspector. It looks as though Lady Simpkins is up to her usual mischief.'

Oh God, he thought not again, and he strode amongst the groups of people, dotted about the lawns, his eyes darting everywhere but to no avail.

'Bloody woman,' he muttered angrily to himself,

'She's probably getting screwed somewhere in the undergrowth . . . Bitch!'

CHAPTER TWENTY THREE

Ginger drove along the quiet lanes leading away from the school and Norman and Charlie followed at a discreet distance. Once again Ginger was driving at a moderate speed, neither too fast nor too slow so as not to attract any unwanted attention. They came to a long deserted stretch which resembled a tunnel, the trees on both sides having grown together over the road. They saw the brake lights of the van and slowed down to pull off the road about a hundred yards behind. They saw Ginger get out of the van, go round to the rear doors and vanish inside. Before stopping he had put on his balaclava once again and he had entered the back of the van so quickly that Samantha had little time in which to react. When she finally realised what was happening she made an attempt to grab at Ginger and remove the mask but wasn't quite quick enough. In a split second he had placed one arm around her, pinning her arms to her sides and with the other hand he was applying black adhesive tape round her eyes to form a blindfold. Next, using the same roll of tape, he placed the woman's hands behind her and fastened them together.

They saw Ginger re-emerge from the van pulling off his balaclava and giving them the "thumbs up" sign and then they were driving again. They crossed over the M4 motorway a little before eleven and drove on towards the farm. The journey was quite uneventful and when they arrived at the farm both the van and the car were driven directly to the barn. Charlie was out of the car in a flash opening the two large doors and when both vehicles were inside Ginger took them quietly to one side and whispered,

'Go inside the both of you and get changed into something old, and Charlie, I suggest that you take a quick shower to remove any traces of that perfume you've been wearing all evening. That Samantha is no fool. I fancy that she is very good at recognising expensive perfumes and you were stood next to her for quite some time this evening. We don't want her making any connections which could link you to all of this if things go wrong. We will let her Ladyship stew for a while. It always makes things a lot easier when the victim is slightly disorientated,' and with that he walked outside into the cooling night air and lit a cigarette.

Norman and Charlie did as Ginger had suggested and as they climbed the stairs in the farmhouse Charlie turned and whispered huskily,

'I think it must be the excitement again. I feel very randy. How do fancy taking a shower with me?'

She lifted the back of her skirt in a very provocative manner giving him a quick glimpse of her lacy stocking tops and the tiny green panties then she ran quickly up the last few stairs. Norman bounded up closely behind her. He was feeling exactly the same and didn't need asking twice. Twenty minutes later they emerged, glowing, from the steaming shower cabinet and it wasn't only as a result of the hot water.

'Ginger will be wondering where the bloody hell we are' said Norman, quickly pulling on a pair of jeans.

'Yes he will . . . and you had better remove that silly grin from your face or he'll know exactly why we've been so long,' she said wriggling into her own jeans.

Back in the barn Ginger was checking that everything was ready to receive their "guest". He had, considerately, made one concession to her femininity by wrapping some soft fleecy material around the leather belt which she would be wearing around her waist during the next few days or even weeks. When Norman and Charlie finally got back he opened the van doors and went inside. Samantha made no move this time. He guided her firmly out of the van and when her feet were firmly on the ground she started to pour out a tirade of abuse and threats.

'Just calm down lassie,' Ginger said soothingly,

'No harm will come to you here. We are not interested in you. You are merely a means to an end . . . a bargaining chip. OK? Now we'll get you settled down for the night,' and he signalled to Charlie to get on with it.

Charlie had always been a good mimic and over the past weeks she had amused herself imitating Norman's flat, northern vowels. She had never done it in front of him of course, only when she was alone, so when she started to speak Norman was both surprised and amused.

She walked over to where Samantha was standing and started,

'Right, let's have them fancy clothes off and get you into something more comfortable.' Norman could hardly believe his ears. She sounded like a completely different person. Charlie led Samantha into the tent and started to cut through the tape binding her arms together.

'It's no good trying anything, not with them two gorillas out there. You might as well get used to th'idea. Yer gonna be here for quite a while.'

She decided not to remove the blindfold for the time being and started to unzip the expensive dress.

'Don't worry luv, I'll take good care of it for you. What you spent on this would keep me in clothes for a year. As the dress slid down Samantha stepped out of it obediently and Charlie looked enviously at the expensive pure silk underwear. Her undies, she thought, had probably cost more than her own entire outfit. She undid the bra and removed it, placing it on the dress which she had folded so carefully. Then she told Samantha to remove her own knickers, she was getting some of the old stirrings as she looked at her beautiful body and was finding it quite disturbing being in such close proximity again, her mind kept flashing back to that day in the showers after the netball match.

'Right, now the stockings and shoes,' she carried on a little breathlessly. Samantha stood there completely naked with her head held high. There was no way she was going to let the humiliation show. Charlie handed her one of the plain pairs of cotton briefs which she had bought in Marks and Spencer and told her to put them on. Next she took the leather belt and fastened it around Samantha's slim waist, making sure that it was tight enough not to be slipped out of, yet comfortable to wear. Then she handed her the disposable pair of overalls. She made Samantha put them on whilst she held the rope attached to the belt, guiding it through the front of them.

She tested the padlock with which she had secured the belt and continued in her phoney northern accent,

'There's plenty o' slack on t' rope so you can get between t' compartments and use t' portable toilet, sit down and eat at t' table and sleep on t' camp bed. In a couple of minutes I'm going to cut away that tape over yer eyes. I'll leave a slip on blindfold and you'll put it on every time before one of us comes into t' tent. If you don't, then, that horrible black tape will be put back on for t' rest of yer stay wi' us. Is that understood?'

Samantha nodded and muttered

'Yes,' with a note of resignation in her voice. She didn't, it seemed, have much choice. She would just have to bide her time . . . after all Humphrey would be pulling out all the stops with his pals at the Home Office, Special Branch and M.I.5 to secure her speedy release. These people will be bound to make some kind of demands sooner or later and then it would just be a matter of time. The one thing that had struck her as odd was that she had not heard an Irish accent. Maybe it was some other lunatic element, but why pick on her? Humphrey was Ministry of Transport for God's sake. Why the hell would anyone choose to kidnap the wife of a Minister in that department? The questions were still whirling round in her mind when she felt Charlie come up behind her and she felt a piece of smooth material being placed in her hand. She could feel Velcro on either end and presumed that this must be the blindfold.

'I'm going to cut the tape now and I'll be using a very sharp Stanley Knife so I advise you to stand perfectly still. As soon as the tape is removed you will put on the blindfold. Is that quite clear? You try and turn round and we might have a nasty accident wi't knife and we wouldn't want to spoil that pretty face now would we?'

Samantha shook her head. No she would comply with everything for now. Perhaps, after a day or two, when she got her bearings and her captors had calmed down a bit she might think of something. Charlie carefully cut through the tape trying not to do too much damage to that marvellous auburn hair.

'This is going to hurt a bit,' she said as she carefully peeled the tape from Samantha's eyes. She had thought, at first, of giving the tape one quick pull as one would with an Elastoplast but decided that it would cause far too much damage to the delicate tissue of the eyelids. The last thing she wanted was to disfigure her old school friend for life. Samantha made no move to turn round until she had put on the blindfold and Charlie had checked it for tightness.

'I think that you should try and get some sleep now. As soon as I leave you can take yon blindfold off and find yer way round yer new home. You'll find everything you need. Sleep tight.' Charlie couldn't resist a little laugh when she thought of the contrast to Samantha's normal standard of living.

'Uncouth, northern bitch,' Samantha muttered to herself as she ripped off the blindfold and made her way to the bed in the other compartment.

CHAPTER TWENTY FOUR

Back inside the farmhouse Norman had made a pot of tea and as Charlie came through the kitchen door he handed her a mug together with a plateful of hot buttered toast.

'Well, how is her Ladyship settling in?' he asked with a grin.

'As well as can be expected,' Charlie retorted, a little sharply.

'I wish to God that I hadn't started that silly Northern accent thing though. I was already finding it very tiresome before I left her and it would be so easy to slip up. I think that either you or Ginger will to have to take her meals for the time being. I've told her about the blindfold routine but you will have to check carefully for the first time or two before you actually go in.'

'OK,' said Norman,

'But our first priority is to decide how we are going to present our demands. Are we going to make our claims over the telephone or are we going to mail one of our little posters direct to Sir Humphrey. Having decided that, do we contact Sir Humphrey at home or at the Ministry? I suggest that we think very seriously about how we make our approach.'

They all sat there in silence, sipping at their steaming hot tea and eating their toast, for ten minutes or more. It was Ginger who spoke first.

'I think that we ought to try both methods simultaneously. We don't want to waste time seeing if one method works before trying the other.'

'My thoughts exactly,' said Norman,

'How about you Charlie, what do you think?'

'I agree, but I don't think that we should do either for twenty four hours. Sir Humphrey and the detective probably won't start getting concerned until the morning. They will assume that Samantha is off on one of her jaunts and will not wish to go public until mid-morning at the earliest. Once they start to realise that she really has gone missing, then we let them stew for a while.'

'Are we all agreed on that?' asked Norman and they all nodded.

'In that case then, we may as well start making preparations first thing in the morning,' and at eight o clock the following day Norman started,

'I will run off some more of the posters and then we can decide where to make the telephone calls from. As Charlie's already pointed out to me, recently, the tracing of calls is alarmingly fast these days. We must never make two calls from the same place and never from within a ten mile radius of this place. I realise that this will entail a lot of driving around the country side but we don't want to make life easy for them. There are three of us so I suggest that we take turns making the calls just to add to their confusion.'

Norman took out an Ordnance Survey map of the area and using a piece of string as a crude compass he drew a circle showing a ten miles radius from the farm. He then started to list places from where the telephone calls could be made. He decided that it would be wise to make the calls from larger towns rather than villages. Most villages, he figured, had only one call box and in small communities people tended to a lot more observant, or to put it more bluntly, nosey.

They all decided that it might be a good idea if they went for a couple of large towns first even if it meant going well outside the ten mile radius. Cheltenham was chosen as the first followed by Oxford and Norman would make the first call.

Norman sat down at the computer in the farm office and pulled up the FORBOR poster file. He added a few more lines of copy at the foot of the page which read:

'Your wife is quite safe, Sir Humphrey, and we assure you that nothing will happen to her providing that we see some evidence of a move to ban heavy lorries from our road system'.

He was wearing the rubber surgical gloves again while he was handling the paper and again when he was addressing the plain white foolscap envelope which he had found in one of the desk drawers. He used a black felt tip pen and wrote in block capitals. The envelope was addressed simply to Sir Humphrey Simpkins, The Ministry of Transport, London. He stuck on a first class stamp and handed it to Charlie who was also wearing gloves now. It had been decided that she would post the letter from the main post office in Bath at the same time as Norman was making the phone call from Cheltenham the following day.

Ginger would be staying at the farm to take care of Samantha, and to get into the swing he had already prepared the day's breakfast of cereal, fresh orange juice and coffee. He had thought of making something more substantial but had decided against it. It would probably be wasted, he thought, she looks like a healthy type that one.

They spent some time during the morning changing the number plates again so that the van now carried its third set since the exercise began. The first meal served to their "guest" had gone fairly smoothly. Ginger had arrived outside the tent carrying the tray and had called through to Samantha and told her to put on the blindfold. She replied that she had done so, but he hadn't taken her word for it. He had looked through a slit in the front of the tent before entering. He placed the tray on the table and left immediately. Almost before he was through the entrance he could hear the click of plastic spoon on dish and realised that she must have been quite hungry having left the previous night's function before the buffet had been served. They had taken the precaution of buying some plastic picnic cutlery just in case she decided to have a go at the rope with her knife.

Norman had taken her lunch in and had also delivered a clean pair of briefs which Charlie had wrapped in a paper bag.

'Are you managing alright with the limited facilities?' he enquired.

'Don't give me all that mock concern you bastard. What the hell do want with me? My husband is quite well off but not loaded. The house in town is mortgaged up to the hilt . . .'

Norman broke in,

'It's not your money we are interested in you stupid woman. Why do your sort always equate everything with money? We have brought you here in order to put some pressure on your husband's Ministry as a part of our campaign to rid our roads of heavy transport.'

'Oh my God, don't tell me I've been hi-jacked by a bunch of loony Greens. You lot make me puke. You drift around the country in your scruffy jeans and your dilapidated vehicles scrounging state benefit. Time you all had a bloody good bath and started looking for jobs. If you were to put half as much energy into a career as you put into your inane protests, you could be millionaires in no time.'

'Have you quite finished,' Norman broke in angrily,

'If you really must know, it's sod all to do with the environment. A few years ago I lost my wife and my two lovely little daughters in a motorway accident as a result of one of those monsters which pound up and down our roads. Some foreign bastard with a gigantic death trap, which had probably not been serviced since new, ploughed into the back of us.'

He broke of, choking back the tears of rage and Samantha said quietly,

'I'm so sorry, I didn't realise, I'm sorry.'

Norman turned quickly before she could say anything else and left the tent. He went outside the barn and lit one of his rare cigarettes and watched his hand shaking as he held the lighter. He was annoyed with himself for spilling it all out in front of the woman. It almost sounded as if he were wallowing in self-pity.

When he got back to the farmhouse Ginger was alone. Charlie had gone to the village for some odds and ends, milk, bread and she had also decided to buy an armful of magazines for Samantha.

'No reason that she should be bored out of her mind while she's being held captive,' she had said on her return from the shop. Norman noted a subtle hint of compassion in her voice whenever she talked about Samantha and wondered to himself, rather cynically, whether they had been more than just good friends at school. He had often heard of the sort of relationships which were formed at boys' public schools. No reason to suppose that it would be any different at a girls' boarding school. It was just a thought, but one worth bearing in mind if things ever came to a showdown.

During the afternoon Norman was busy on his own. He had taken the explosive devices from the van and was placing them at strategic positions around the farm. He placed one on either side of the entrance gate, he put another at the foot of the wooden pole which carried the electricity supply to the house and he also buried one in the gravel drive leading down to the barn. He hoped that he would never need to detonate them but he had learned from Ginger that it always paid to have something up your sleeve in an emergency.

After they had eaten their evening meal, Ginger took a tray down to a very subdued Samantha and when he got back to the house, they sat down with a can of lager apiece and went over the plans for the following day once more.

CHAPTER TWENTY FIVE

An uneventful night shift at Chippenham police station was just coming to an end when a bedraggled young man in evening dress walked in. He looked as if he had been sleeping under a hedge but when he spoke it was with a very upper crust accent.

Oh, great, thought Sergeant Bamford, this I could do without at this time of day. Another Hooray Henry who's got pissed out of his mind and can't find his car or his wallet or his keys. Bloody irresponsible lot. more money than sense.

'I should like to report an assault and a kidnapping,' said Tarquin Barrington, trying to sound dignified despite his dishevelled appearance.

'Very good Sir, then we'd better take down some details,' said the Sergeant with a sigh of exasperation.

'Just who has been assaulted and who has

been kidnapped,' he continued as if speaking to a small child.

'I'm not sure that I like your tone Sergeant. May I remind you that I came in to make a complaint and that I should like to be taken seriously.'

'Yes of course Sir, now if we can get on . . . Name?'

'Tarquin Barrington,' the sergeant tried to suppress a smirk but didn't quite succeed.

Have I said something to amuse you Sergeant?'

' No of course not sir and your address?'

The sergeant continued to take down details in a laboured manner assuming that this was just another jolly jape that had gone further than intended until the name Lady Samantha Simpkins was mentioned. The young man, quite self-centred like most of his ilk, had concentrated first and foremost on the assault upon himself and had then started to give details of the kidnap, almost as an afterthought.

What time did you say that all this happened Sir?'

I've told you, between about nine thirty and ten.'

Then why have you taken so long to report the matter?' Sergeant Bamford was beginning to take it all seriously now. He had heard that there was an important couple from London at Queensbridge girls' school the previous evening, but his understanding was that they had their own police protection with them. The local constabulary had not been requested to make any special arrangements, but he was already thinking ahead in case he had to start covering his own arse when everything hit the fan, which it would if her Ladyship really had been abducted.

Because, Sergeant, this thug who came up behind us and grabbed Samantha dealt me a particularly savage blow to the throat. I must have been out for hours. Dawn was breaking when I came to the first time then I must have passed out again for the next thing I knew it was broad daylight. I have walked all the way here from the grounds of Queensbridge. No one would give me a lift, hardly surprising when you consider the state that I'm in. So, now that I am finally here, what are you going to do about it?'

'Right Sir, you said he came up behind US.

Who else was present when the alleged kidnap took place?'

Tarquin noted the subtle change in interest from the assault on himself to the kidnap of Samantha.

'Well, that's just it. I don't really know who they were. We weren't formally introduced you understand but, Samantha appeared to know the girl quite well, but as for the chap who was with her, I have no idea. A Northerner by the sound of it. Didn't really seem to fit in.'

'I see. Did you happen to hear what either of them was called? We will have to speak to both of them. It would be useful if had a name or names to start with.'

'I'm sorry Sergeant, I'm afraid I can't help you. I wasn't really taking that much interest. Not my types, either of them. All I was really interested was getting Samantha somewhere alone. Do you get my drift Sergeant,' Tarquin said with an exaggerated wink as he tapped the side of his nose with a long, well manicured finger.

'Oh yes Sir, I get your drift all right. I know exactly what you were interested in. However you are going to have to do much better than that. I suggest that you take a seat in the interview room over there and think very hard about what happened last night and who, if anyone, also witnessed this kidnap. Meanwhile I will contact someone in CID. I have no doubt that they will have many more questions to ask,' and with that he led Tarquin, protesting, to the room across the passage and told a young constable to sit in with him.

He immediately got on to Detective Superintendent Fellows and gave him details of what the young chap had just told him.

'OK George, I'll be right down. Where is he now?'

'Interview room No. 1 sir,' and he slowly replaced the receiver. Bloody hell, he thought, why did this have to happen today of all days. George Bamford and his wife had made plans to have a few days break down in Cornwall, but if this blew up into a full scale kidnap investigation then all leave would be cancelled for sure.

While this was going on in Chippenham, Sir Humphrey was just finishing breakfast which had been brought up to his hotel room. Inspector Barnes sat in one of the armchairs in the well appointed suite and waited. He knew from bitter experience not to interrupt Sir Humphrey during his breakfast. Most important meal of the day, Barnes, he had said on numerous occasions.

Finally Sir Humphrey put down his copy of the Times and dabbed the corner of his mouth with the starched linen napkin.

'Well as you can see Inspector, her Ladyship did not grace us with her presence last night. Start the usual discreet enquiries. Police, hospitals . . . you know the routine. If you draw a blank then you had better get down to the school and see if anyone can remember who she was last seen with. Remember, discretion is the key word as always. I'm terribly sorry about this Barnes. I am afraid that Lady Samantha's behaviour is becoming quite intolerable.'

'I'll get on it right away Sir, and don't worry we'll have her back safely in the fold by lunchtime,' and he went over to the telephone on the desk in the large bay window. He tried the hospitals first just in case there had been an accident of some kind but with no success. Well at least she's still in one piece he thought. He decided to call the police station in Chippenham next but, by the time he rang, Sergeant Bamford had already left for home and hopefully for a short break in Cornwall. The day Sergeant looked quickly through the incident book but saw no mention of a Lady Simpkins and reported the same to Barnes.

'No luck I take it Inspector,' Sir Humphrey was already packing his small suitcase and stuffing papers into his ancient briefcase.

'Afraid not Sir, but I have left a message with the desk Sergeant at Chippenham to ring me here should he hear anything.'

Back at the police station Detective Superintendent Fellows was passing the front desk when the Sergeant looked up and enquired,

'Does the name Lady Samantha Simpkins mean anything to you Sir?'

'Why do ask, Sergeant,' Fellows asked, trying to keep the surprise out of his voice.

'Well Sir, an Inspector Barnes rang about ten minutes ago asking if we had seen or heard anything of the lady. He seemed a bit cagey like . . . didn't want to give anything away but I could tell from his voice that he was anxious to track her down.'

'Thanks very much Sergeant. Did the Inspector leave a number on which you could contact him?'

'Yes Sir, he did. Do you want me to ring him back?'

'Yes Sergeant! Please ask Inspector Barnes to come to the station as soon as possible and bring him up to my office as soon as he arrives.'

Very interesting, Fellows thought as he climbed the stairs to his first floor office. Maybe this chap Tarquin was telling the truth after all. It had all seemed a little far-fetched when he had listened to the story. That sort of thing might be commonplace in London and other large cities, but this was Chippenham, nice, all for a quiet life Chippenham. Why the hell couldn't these Government Ministers stay in London and let the Met' deal with all their problems. He didn't need the aggravation on his patch.

Quarter of an hour later Inspector Barnes arrived and the desk Sergeant showed him up to the Superintendent's office. Fellows indicated a chair,

'Please, take a seat Inspector and tell me what your interest is in Lady Simpkins.'

'This is a rather delicate matter Sir. I am a member of the Political Protection Squad at present assigned to Sir Humphrey and Lady Simpkins. He is Under Secretary of State at the Ministry of Transport as you probably know and gives us absolutely no cause for anxiety. Her Ladyship, however, is a different matter altogether. She has the habit of going missing. Going off on wild sprees despite my best efforts. In the squad we have to tread a very thin line between maintaining security and making virtual prisoners of our wards. Of course, Lady Samantha realises this and plays on it and she tends to shrug off any warnings made by Sir Humphrey and myself. Last night was a case in point. She and Sir Humphrey were guests of honour at the annual Prize Giving out at Queensbridge School for Girls. It was a warm evening as you know and many of the guests were out in the grounds once the dancing began. I was keeping an eye on her quite successfully as I thought until a breathless little girl came up to me and told me that Sir Humphrey wanted me inside the school hall immediately. Lady Samantha seemed to be engrossed in conversation with a young blonde girl and two men. She didn't appear to be going anywhere . . I've learnt to spot the signs over the years, so I went in, only to find that I wasn't wanted at all. When I rushed back outside there was no sign of her or the people she had been talking to. I managed to track down the little girl who had spoken to me and asked her if Lady Samantha had asked her to deliver the bogus message. Oh no, she had replied, quite emphatically, it wasn't a lady it was a man. He had a Scottish accent and the most amazing ginger coloured hair.'

'The two men she was talking to Inspector, can you describe them?'

'Yes Sir. One was about five foot ten, dark brown hair, a largish nose and was wearing a black dinner jacket with a green bow tie. The other was about six foot two with a shock of blonde hair again in evening dress with a black bow tie.'

Interesting thought Fellows. The description of the second man fitted Tarquin Barrington to a "T" but he didn't betray any interest in either description and just as an aside he added,

'And the girl, what did she look like?'

'Aged about twenty or so, blonde hair, about five foot eight and she was wearing the most stunning, short green dress.'

'I see,' said Fellows, his tone turning suddenly

very serious,

'I'm afraid that I may have some alarming news for you Inspector.'

CHAPTER TWENTY SIX

Samantha was settling into a routine now. She had determined not to give way to anger and frustration but instead had calmed down. She was being treated quite well considering her surroundings and was now well down the pile of magazines which Charlie had provided. The food, whilst not exactly "Haute Cuisine" was always served hot, fresh and was reasonably appetising. The washing facilities were, to say the least, primitive but they were adequate. Having said that she would have killed for the chance to take a shower.

She was seated at the table with her magazines and started to wonder how Humphrey was taking all of this. It was now the second day and she was completely ignorant of what was happening. Had they made any demands yet? If so how would Humphrey react? He would be very careful. That would be his immediate reaction. Careful. He would do nothing which would harm his precious career. He would play everything very close to his chest and going public would be the very last resort. Poor old Barnes would be running around in circles trying to find out what had happened to her. Humphrey would be on his back every hour of the day . . . she could hear him now . . . 'Discretion is the key word Barnes, this must be treated on a strictly "need to know" basis'. Poor old Barnes. She wasn't particularly fond of the man but, in fairness, he had always had her safety and well-being at heart. He would be approaching the problem in his usual methodical manner and Samantha had no doubt that if there were clues to be found, Barnes was the man to do it. Yes, it would only be matter of time before her whereabouts were discovered.

It was almost mid-day and she heard one of the large barn doors being opened. Which one of them would be bringing her lunch today she wondered? Would it be the brusque Scotsman or the pathetic Northerner? Despite her predicament she had felt quite sorry for the man who had lost everything, wife, little girls, and even a reason to go on living. What he had gone through was enough to drive anyone into doing something desperate but he had gone on living, driven, possibly by some overwhelming sense of guilt at having survived the accident himself or perhaps the need for some kind of revenge.

Ginger approached the tent and shouted,

'Have you got yon blindfold on lassie?'

'Of course,' came back the reply in that upper class accent. Samantha was tempted to leave the thing off and have a look at the man but resisted. She wasn't sure what kind of reprisals such an action would provoke so she kept it on, but just for devilment she undid the zip on her overall almost down to the waist just to see what sort of a reaction it would cause.

Ginger took in the tray and the unzipped overall wasn't lost on him. However he was too much of a professional to be distracted by such things,

'You'll catch your death of cold lassie, better do that thing up,' he placed her tray on the table, turned and walked out without another word.

Ignorant Celtic bastard she thought but that clearly ruled out the Scot as far as using sex as a weapon was concerned. Perhaps she might have more success with the other one. Maybe he would be more vulnerable to something like that. After all, he had lost his wife four years ago and she very much doubted that he had been with another woman since then. The guilt, she was sure, would have been too much for him.

Norman was already in Cheltenham, having set off just after ten. He had parked the Transit on a car park in Albion Street, close to the town centre and had walked to the post office on Royal Well Road just opposite the top of the same street. It was quiet, being Sunday morning, and he entered the end box of a row of four. He dialled the number for directory enquiries and asked for the number of Mrs Samantha Simpkins, Eaton Place, London. There was a short delay and Norman suddenly had the horrible feeling that the Simpkins might well be ex-directory. As it happened his fears were unfounded . . . the operator came back with the number which he jotted down and quickly replaced the receiver. Seconds later the London number was ringing out and after three or four seconds the upper crust voice of Sir Humphrey answered with a curt,

'Yes,'

'Is that Sir Humphrey Simpkins?'

'Yes, who is this please?'

'Never mind who this is, just listen. My code word is FORBOR. That probably means nothing to you at the moment but, I assure you, it will. If you want to see your wife again listen very carefully. Once we hear an announcement that the Government is planning to ban all vehicles over twenty tons in weight from our roads and put freight back on the railways, your wife will be released completely unharmed.'

He banged down the receiver to the sound of Sir Humphrey's protests, his hands were shaking and his brow was running with sweat. He went round the corner and into the nearest pub which had just opened its doors. He ordered a double Scotch and downed it in one. He ordered another and went to sit down in an alcove by the window. He could feel the first drink warming its way down but he was still shaking. The pub was filling up now and he decided to leave and start the drive back to the farm. No point hanging around. The longer he was in the town the more the chance that someone would remember seeing him or the van.

Meanwhile, Charlie was walking from the car park in Beaumont Street to the post office in St.

Michaels Street. It was very quiet in Oxford on this still Autumn Sunday morning. She was wearing jeans and a leather jacket and looked like just another student out for a walk. She decided, after posting the letter, to have a walk down to the river and watch the punts. It was so different from her University in Manchester which was set in the middle of a rather squalid urban area which was populated by many different ethnic groups. As she walked past the ancient colleges built of the local creamy coloured stone she felt slightly envious. Had she done better with her 'A' levels she might have come here and things would have turned out very differently. For the first time since she had met Norman Parker she was starting to have serious doubts about what she had got mixed up in. She loved Norman but they were getting into this thing quite deeply now and even if they were to release Samantha today, the authorities wouldn't let the matter drop. They would keep on relentlessly until they found the culprits.

She stood on the bridge over the Cherwell and watched carefree couples gliding along on the dark green water alongside the overhanging willow trees and she shivered despite the warm sun on her back. After a while she turned and made her way reluctantly back to the car park. The letter which she had posted with gloved hands was on its way now and would probably land on the Simpkins door mat the following morning. She climbed into the car with a strange feeling of impending doom.

She drove quite fast once she had cleared the town. The windows were wound down in an effort to blow away this mood which had overcome her. She turned the radio up and by the time she had reached Burford and turned onto the A361 back towards the farm she was feeling much more cheerful. Now she was anxious to get back and find out how Norman had got on.

Norman had just put the van back in the barn and was walking up to the house as Charlie came down the drive. He ran the last few yards and greeted her with a hug as she got out of the car.

'How did it go?' she asked still clinging to him.

'It was bloody nerve racking. I've only just stopped shaking. It's one thing planning these things but when you are actually talking to the woman's husband it's a bit scary. I have been going over it again and again on the way back. I think that I said everything we agreed, in fact, yes, I'm sure I did. How did you get on? I thought that you would have been back before me.'

'I would have been, said Charlie,

But I decided to go for a walk around the place. I walked down to the river. We will have to go there, when all this is over, and take out a punt. It all looked so peaceful.'

'Do you think that was wise, staying there longer than you needed to?'

'Oh come on Norman, don't let's carried away. Who the hell do you think was taking any notice of me walking around Oxford on a Sunday morning. for Christ's sake, you're getting bloody paranoid.'

'I'm sorry. I suppose I am but it is so often the little things that trip people up. Come on let's go inside and have a drink and see how Ginger's been getting on.'

Ginger greeted them as they went into the kitchen,

'Tea, or something stronger?'

'Tea will be fine,' they answered in unison,

'And how was your day?'

'Oh, little miss hot pants down there tried flashing her boobs at me . . . what the hell she thought that might achieve I really don't know.'

'Oh, come on, you know damn well,' chuckled Charlie,

'Don't try and tell me that you weren't tempted.'

'I well, that's as may be lassie. Under different circumstances maybe I would, but we are here to do a job and you know what they say. Never mix pleasure with business!'

CHAPTER TWENTY SEVEN

When Inspector Barnes heard what Fellows had to say about the suspected abduction of Lady Samantha he had felt physically sick. The one thing he had been dreading since taking over his present assignment had actually happened. Sir Humphrey would go mad when he found out. After grilling Tarquin Barrington for over an hour he left Chippenham police station and headed immediately for the hotel.

'Well Barnes, what's the story?' Sir Humphrey was pacing up and down the spacious suite.

Barnes began to relate all the facts he had learned from the police in Chippenham and Sir Humphrey got more and more agitated.

'My God man, how did you allow this to happen? If anything happens to Samantha I'll have your balls in a vice. If you somehow manage to remain in the force, I'll see to it that you finish up directing traffic in some God forsaken backwater.'

Barnes continued, calmly, telling his boss what he thought they should do next. He was rather surprised at the outburst but he had too much to organise to dwell on it.

'I think that we should get back to Eaton Place at once Sir. There is a lot to prepare before the kidnappers make their demands. They may even have tried already . . . the answer phone is switched on isn't it.'

It was a rhetorical question and he continued quickly without waiting for an answer,

'Let's get your things down to the car right away and get underway. We should make reasonable time back to London, it being a Saturday,' and with that he picked up the suitcases and followed Sir Humphrey down to the lobby. Within minutes of settling the account they were in the car and were soon joining the east bound traffic on the M4.

Just before mid-day they were mounting the steps of the house in Eaton Square and as Barnes unlocked the front door the phone was ringing. He rushed into the drawing room and snatched up the receiver only to find one of Sir Humphrey's minions on the other end of the line cancelling one many his appointments for the following Monday morning. Sir Humphrey took the phone from Barnes and told the middle aged spinster to cancel ALL his appointments for the foreseeable future. He gave no reason and the lady knew from the tone of his voice not to query the instruction.

The minute the phone was free Barnes was on to one of his contacts at the Anti-Terrorism Branch to see if anyone there had heard anything on the grapevine regarding the abduction of Lady Samantha. He was told that nothing had surfaced so far. However, his contact had told him that there had been a new organisation flagged up on the computer a couple of days ago. He asked Barnes if the name FORBOR meant anything to him, and whether there been anything left at the scene of the abduction, a small poster for instance.

'No, nothing like that,' said Barnes,

'Why do you say that? Is there something that I should know about this new outfit?'

'Well it may be nothing but this FORBOR lot have been involved in a couple of incidents in the West Midlands and are making demands regarding the removal of heavy goods vehicles from the road system. As your boss is Ministry of Transport, I think that it is an avenue worth exploring, after all, it is all too easy these days to assume that anything that happens is automatically down to our Irish friends.'

'Yes I suppose you're right, we should keep an open mind until we receive some communication from whoever is responsible,' Barnes's mind was racing. He replaced the phone and immediately picked it up again, this time contacting British Telecom special services. He would require the most sophisticated equipment available for the instant tracing of any calls which may ensue.

Samantha had been quite wrong about her husband's reaction to the kidnapping. He was very fond of her, deep down. He wasn't a very demonstrative sort of man. Years at Public School had put paid to that sort of thing. Stiff upper lip and all that. But now he was openly distraught and Barnes didn't really know how to cope with this new side of Sir Humphrey. He was starting to feel quite sorry for the man and didn't know quite how to react. He was far more used to the abrasive, overbearing side of his boss's nature.

Within a quarter of an hour the drawing room was filled with engineers from Telecom who were busy installing strange looking boxes, computer screens and miles of cable. If anyone phoned the house now, the location of the caller would be pinpointed within seconds.

The afternoon dragged on into early evening without incident. Barnes had called out for some take-away food and an hour later the foil trays lay around the large coffee table, most of their contents still intact. Neither of the men had felt particularly hungry when it had come down to it. They were both equally concerned about the fate of Samantha. Barnes was surprised to note that his concern was actually for her Ladyship and not, as had previously been the case, for his pension. Both men sat staring at the telephone each nursing a large goblet of fine brandy and it was after midnight when Barnes suggested that they should take it in turns to sleep. Barnes said that he would take the first watch and settled back into his armchair with one of the glossy magazines from the rack beneath the coffee table. Sir Humphrey tossed and turned on the massive four-seater settee and after an hour or so finally submitted to his exhaustion.

Poor old bastard, Barnes thought, he really does care for her. One would never have guessed it from the way each of them behaved when they were together. He wondered whether she held him in the same regard. Somehow he doubted it, she was a flighty bitch.

He had let Sir Humphrey sleep on. He hadn't had the heart to rouse him . . . better to let him get all the rest he could. He was going to need it if this situation was to drag on, and he was in no doubt that it would. Around eight o clock in the morning he went into the kitchen and made some strong black coffee. He binned the smelly remains of the take-away and suddenly he was very hungry.

Sir Humphrey came suddenly awake aware of the smell of bacon and eggs frying. Barnes pressed a cup of black coffee into his hands as he sat up flexing his aching muscles.

'Fancy some breakfast Sir,' Barnes was trying his best to sound cheerful but he knew that he wasn't fooling anyone.

'Thank you Barnes, you're a good chap. I'm sorry for the way I railed off at you yesterday.

Not your fault . . . I know that Samantha is difficult to keep an eye on, even for a professional like yourself. I do care for her a lot you know Barnes. I realise that you wouldn't think so to listen to us sometimes.'

'I do understand Sir. Eggs and bacon or just a little toast perhaps? Have to keep up our strength.'

'Quite right Barnes, look I can't keep calling you Barnes, not in the circumstances. What's your first name'?

'Harry, Sir.'

'Right, Harry, eggs and bacon sounds great. Have you eaten yet?'

'Yes, thank you Sir,' he could see the lines of worry which were creasing Sir Humphrey's face and knew that he was just trying to put on a brave face. The good old stiff upper lip syndrome. It was at times like this that Barnes was glad that he hadn't been condemned to the public school system where it was considered terribly bad form to reveal one's feelings.

He cleared away the breakfast pots and stuck them in the dishwasher before going down to the news stand for the Sunday Papers. Later in the morning while they were both staring at, but not actually reading, their respective papers, the phone rang. Harry Barnes leapt across to one of the screens which had been installed and put on a pair of earphones and nodded to Sir Humphrey to pick up the phone.

Sir Humphrey place the phone to his ear,

'Yes'!

'Is that Sir Humphrey Simpkins?'

'Yes, who is this please?'

'Never mind who this is, just listen. My code word is FORBOR. That probably means nothing to you at the moment but, I assure you, it will. Once we hear an announcement that the Government is planning to ban all vehicles over twenty tons in weight from our roads and put freight back on the railways, your wife will be released completely unharmed.'

There was a loud click and the dialling tone returned through the earpiece.

'You won't get away with this you swine . . .' but Sir Humphrey was shouting to himself and he slammed down the receiver, close to tears.

While the conversation was taking place Barnes was watching intently as a series of numbers was appearing on the screen in front of him. As soon as the number was completed the screen started to scroll information at an alarming rate. Suddenly the scrolling ceased and one line of information started to flash. It revealed the location of a public call box in the town of Cheltenham. He picked up the telephone and dialled the number of the central police station in the town.

Within minutes of the call two police cars where speeding towards the phone box on Royal Well Road but when they arrived there was no one to be seen. Shortly afterwards Norman Parker crossed the road towards the car park glancing nervously at the cars parked by the Post Office with their blue and red lights flashing urgently. He tried desperately not quicken his pace as he headed for the van. That would have been a fatal mistake. Ginger had always drummed it in to him that movement, especially any quick movement was a dead give- away when being pursued.

CHAPTER TWENTY EIGHT

After a good Sunday lunch Charlie went down to the barn to collect Samantha's plastic plate and cutlery. She had decided to have a look for herself and see how her old school friend was bearing up. After all, there would be no need to speak and therefore no risk of a lapse from that silly Northern accent she had adopted on the first day. Of course, as soon as she stood outside the tent she realised that she would in fact have to speak in order to ensure that Samantha was wearing the blindfold.

'Have you got that blindfold on, lady?' she shouted using flat, broad vowels.

'Just a moment,' came back the upper class reply,

'OK, you can come in now,' Samantha was getting to the stage now when she welcomed any human contact, even the company of this uncouth young woman. Charlie walked into the tent and went over to the table where Samantha was still sitting. She looked down at her friend and was amazed how good she looked. Her lovely auburn hair was tied up into a pony tail and although she wore no make-up, she still managed to look quite beautiful. Even the cheap, disposable overall she wore somehow managed to look like a fashionable garment on her. She really was incredible, determined not to let her standards fall, even in the most dire of circumstances. For a brief moment Charlie was tempted to speak to her in her normal voice and offer some sort of assurance that she would come to no harm, but she stopped herself just in time. Good friends or not, once she had let her guard drop, she would be the only one of the trio who could be identified when all this was over and she had no desire to carry the can all by herself. She gathered up the plate and utensils and left quickly. She had a very uneasy feeling as she walked back up to the farmhouse and it was not lost on Norman as she walked into the kitchen.

'You alright, love?' he took the things from her and there was concern in his voice.

Although the idea of kidnapping Samantha had come originally from Charlie, he had always been worried that, when the chips were down, she may do something silly. Women tended to think with their hearts not their heads in some situations. He knew that was a very chauvinist attitude but, nevertheless it was true. He would have to keep a close eye on her reactions. He loved her very much but he could not allow her to jeopardise the whole enterprise because of misplaced loyalties.

'Yes, I'm perfectly alright,' and she could have bitten her tongue off as she heard the cold tone of dismissal in her voice.

'I'm sorry,' she said with a hint of contrition in her voice,

'I know this was all my idea but I feel awful seeing her being kept prisoner like that.'

'I do understand, love. Maybe you should leave visits to the barn to Ginger and me in future. No point upsetting yourself by continuing to go down there. It's no problem. Now let's see where you are going to make your phone call from tomorrow morning,' and with that he spread out the Ordnance Survey map on the large kitchen table.

They decided on the small town of Marlborough for the next call. It was in a totally different direction from the first call and although it was in the general southerly direction of Chippenham, it was far enough to the west so as not matter.

After breakfast on Monday morning Charlie driven off in Norman's car and headed for Marlborough. She arrived just after nine and selected a public phone box at random. She dialled the London number and after three rings it was answered by Sir Humphrey. He sounded tired and worried,

'Yes,' his voice had lost its usual edge.

'Is that Sir Humphrey Simpkins?' she said in her best upper class accent.

'Yes, who is this,' it could, he thought, have been anyone, a friend of Samantha's, someone from the office, it was that sort of voice.

'Never mind who this is. Code word FORBOR. Have you or your department done anything about our demand yet?'

'Look young lady I wish to speak to my wife. I really'

'You really MUST listen,' she broke in,

'And act very quickly if you wish to see your

wife again. If we don't hear an announcement before six this evening, to the effect that the government intend to ban all Killer Juggernauts from our roads, then you will only have yourself to blame.'

The phone went dead in his hand and he turned to Barnes with a helpless look on his face.

'Try not to worry Sir,' Barnes said not taking his eyes from the rapidly scrolling screen of his computer.

'The call was from a public box in Marlborough.'

He tapped the letters M-A-R-L into another computer by his elbow. This one contained the number of every police station in the country and within seconds it flashed up the required number in Marlborough. He picked up the phone, dialled and within two minutes a patrol car was hurrying to the call box. Charlie sat in her car about fifty yards away and watched as the police car screeched to a halt. They are certainly well organised, she thought. Sir Humphrey must be pulling out all the stops. It was a little frightening to see just how efficient they were. Her thoughts were disturbed as she saw a young constable walking towards the car.

'Good morning Miss,' Charlie had wound down the window as he approached.

'Have you been here long?'

Charlie's mouth was dry but she answered as confidently as she could,

'About five minutes. I'm waiting for the dry cleaners to open at half past,' she was almost convinced herself it sounded so plausible.

'Did you happen to see anyone using the telephone box over there by any chance?'

'Yes, as a matter of fact I did, a very striking lady in a long black dress was just coming out of the box as I parked. She went up the alley over there. I wouldn't have taken much notice had it not been for the dress. It really was very smart.'

'Thanks very much Miss, you've been very helpful,' and he raced back towards the police car signalling to his colleague as he ran. She waited until the two of them had disappeared up the alley before starting the car and she was soon heading back northwards and she crossed the M4 by Swindon about ten o clock.

Back in the house in Eaton Square, Harry Barnes was just receiving the news from

Marlborough police station that they had drawn a blank. A women in a black dress had been seen leaving the phone box minutes before the patrol car arrived but no trace had been found of the woman. Hardly surprising as she had never existed in the first place. Barnes picked up the phone again and dialled the number of Detective Superintendent Laidlow in the West Midlands. It was he who had flagged up the name FORBOR on the police computer and he wanted to get all the information he could on the group. A quarter of an hour later when he replaced the phone he wasn't much wiser. Laidlow had told him about the two explosions on the M5 and about the yellow posters which had been found at the scene, posters which sounded identical to the letter which they had received. But it appeared that the trail had gone cold. Laidlow had traced a probable source of the paper used for the posters but there was nothing conclusive. Barnes had made a few notes during the conversation, yellow Transit van . . . attractive young blonde . . . professional explosive devices . . . none of which seemed to be of any use in the present situation. He had appraised Bill Laidlow of the kidnap of Lady Samantha and of the phone calls and the letter which had been received and had been promised full cooperation from the West Midlands Anti-Terrorism Squad. He stressed, as if he needed to, the importance of keeping any of this information from the media. He decided to pay a visit to the area around Swindon. A pattern was emerging. The source of the phone calls, the place where the letter had been posted, the actual kidnap all appeared to be within a crude circle and Swindon was pretty close to being the centre of that circle. Perhaps if he visited the area he might get a feel for the place and hopefully some inspiration. Of course he knew the old maxim about police work. "10% inspiration . . . 90% perspiration", but it was worth a try. He certainly wasn't getting very far sat here in Eaton Square. He arranged for a constable who was well versed in the call tracing equipment to stay with Sir Humphrey whilst he was away. He left strict instructions that he must be contacted immediately if there was any further contact from the kidnappers. He didn't really like the thought of leaving Sir Humphrey in his present state of mind but he managed to convince him to stay put and be ready to receive any further phone calls He assured him that the constable would make contact with himself the minute anything happened. An hour later he was on the M4 heading for the Post House Hotel on the outskirts of Swindon where he would set up his temporary headquarters for the next few days.

CHAPTER TWENTY NINE

When Charlie got back to the farm she and Norman decided to go down to the local for a spot of lunch and a couple of beers. Ginger had received a phone call during the morning and he had returned to London on urgent business. Norman said that he had looked a little fraught after the call and had said very little as he had thrown his few belongings into a bag and driven off.

The weather was changing now and it felt more like autumn as they walked over the fields to the village. The overnight dew still lay on the grass and before they were halfway there they were beginning to wish they had taken the slightly longer route via the road. The leaves of the hawthorn bushes were starting to turn a yellowy brown colour and the horse chestnuts were suddenly prematurely bare.

They reached the pub to find it already quite full but found a table in one of the small bay windows. After ordering a couple of pints of lager they decided on the "special" for the day, home-made steak and kidney pie. The food arrived piping hot and as they started to eat Norman asked,

'How did it go this morning? What sort of response did you get? Were you able to gauge his mood?'

'Hang on. One question at a time,' she said sucking in copious amounts of air to cool the food in her mouth.

'To be honest I wasn't on the line long enough to gauge anything. I was so bloody nervous I just said my piece, rang off and got back to the car as quickly as I could. Just as well as it happened. I'd hardly sat down when a police car came screaming up to the telephone box. They must have some pretty fancy equipment to be able to pinpoint the phone and then get the local cops round in such a short time. I don't mind admitting I was a bit scared, especially when the young policeman came over to speak to me.'

'Why did he pick on you for God's sake?'

Norman sounded worried.

'Probably because I was the only one in the street who was actually sitting in a car. There weren't all that many cars around anyway. I gave him a cock and bull story about waiting for the dry cleaners to open and then sent him and his colleague off on a wild goose chase after a non-existent woman in a black dress.'

They finished the rest of their meal in comparative silence then ordered another two pints which they drank as they chatted, a little more relaxed now. It was almost three o clock as they left and as they walked back, along the road this time, Charlie squeezed Norman's hand and said,

'I gave them an ultimatum. They make some sort of announcement before six this evening or else.'

'Or else what for Christ sake. That was a bloody silly thing to do. That puts US on the spot now. They will just sit tight, call our bluff and I don't think that either of us is prepared to do anything to harm Samantha. That was never part of the plan.'

'I'm sorry Norman. I panicked and said the first thing that came into my head. I've made a right mess of things haven't I?'

'Well all we can do now is sit tight with the television on and just hope for a miracle,' he squeezed her hand now as they walked on in silence. Back at the farm they switched on the television and left it playing quietly on ITV channel 3. Charlie disappeared into the kitchen to prepare an evening meal for Samantha. If there was no announcement, which seemed likely, she doubted whether either of them would fancy eating much but there was no reason for Samantha to go hungry.

When Norman had taken the food down to the barn he asked as he came back through the door,

'Anything on the early news?' He had a horrible feeling that there wouldn't have been. Even if Sir Humphrey was considering complying with their demands there would not have been time for any decision to have been taken at government level. In any event, the chances of that decision being taken were pretty remote given the government's tacit refusal in the past to succumb to terrorist threats. He began to wonder why on earth he had agreed to embark on the kidnapping in the first place.

'No, nothing,' Charlie said contritely,

'You never expected there would be did you? I'm sorry I've made such a mess of everything. What on earth do we do now?'

'God knows,' Norman sounded worried,

If we had any bloody sense we would just turn her free and make a run for it, but having come so far I think that we should give it just one more go. I'll ring again in the morning and try and put the fear of God up them.'

The atmosphere was pretty tense during the evening and as soon as they listened to the headlines on News at Ten they retired for the night.

The following morning Norman was up first and had started to make breakfast by the time Charlie appeared. I'll take Samantha's food down and then get off to Burford to make the phone call.

Meanwhile down in the barn Samantha had decided on a course of action. If it was the Northerner who brought her breakfast this morning she was going to try a little seduction. Even if it didn't achieve anything positive it could prove to be quite an amusing interlude, after all, she wasn't used to going so long without a bit of sex. When Humphrey was busy, which was most of the time, she always managed to find someone with whom she could enjoy a little diversion. She would tell the Northerner that she was just showing how grateful she was for him having brought the heater last night. Norman had found a Calor gas heater in one of the spare bedrooms and had taken it down to the tent. Although the barn was well insulated with all the bales of straw, nevertheless it was getting decidedly cooler at night recently. He had also found two full bottles of gas in one of the out houses and he didn't see any reason why the lass should be cold at nights.

Norman shouted out as he approached the tent with the breakfast tray,

'Have you got the blindfold on?'

Just a moment . . . right you can come in now"!

The tent was lovely and warm and as he walked over to place the tray on the table a husky voice called out from the other compartment,

'I'm in here sweetie,' so Norman, thinking that she had only just woken, took the tray through. As he went into the section which served as a bedroom he almost dropped the tray. Samantha was lying on the bed wearing only the blindfold and the leather belt around her waist. She looked absolutely devastating. She lay there with her hands behind her head, her well-formed breasts standing proud. She had one knee bent and her legs were slightly parted. Norman's eyes were riveted on her neatly trimmed bikini line, the little wisps of curly down were the same startling auburn colour as her hair.

'Put the tray down and come here,' she had heard the contents of the tray rattling as Norman's hands shook.

He put the tray carefully down on the ground and just stood there staring.

'How about we take off this horrible belt, it could get in the way,' Norman swallowed hard, not knowing how to react. Surely it wouldn't do any harm to play along he thought. He walked over to the bed and as he got closer he could smell the musky scent of her body and he was getting very aroused. He bent over her and removed the heavy leather belt and as he did so she put her arms around his neck and pulled him down to her. Her hands then worked quickly on the belt of his jeans and in no time he had on only his T shirt, she had obviously done this sort of thing many times before.

Soon they were locked together in a series of overwhelming spasms of pleasure. She was totally abandoned. Norman had thought that Charlie was pretty wild when they made love but this was something else. As he climaxed he felt all the suspense and frustration of the last couple of days drain out of him. Samantha was insatiable, she clung around his neck determined that he would not pull away from her as she went from one writhing orgasm to the next.

Back in the house, Charlie had finished her bowl of cereal and drained her coffee cup. She stood up and looked out of the window. Norman's taking a long time to deliver Samantha's breakfast, she thought as she placed her pots in the dishwasher. Ten minutes later he had still not returned and curiosity got the better of her. She walked down to the barn fully expecting to see Norman backing the van out of the barn. He was going to use the van to go up to Burford while she took the car up to the supermarket in Cirencester to pick up some groceries.

There was no sign as she rounded the corner

and she continued on into the barn. As she approached the tent she could hear the sounds of their sexual exertions. She crept nearer and quietly lifted the flap of the tent door. She couldn't believe her eyes as she peered into the section which served as Samantha's bedroom. They were locked together completely unaware of her presence. She clasped her hand over her mouth to stop the scream of anger and rushed from the barn, tears streaming down her face.

You rotten two timing bastard,' she screamed as soon as she was clear of the barn and she ran blindly towards the house.

CHAPTER THIRTY

Harry Barnes had booked into the Post House Hotel in Swindon just after mid-day. He made two phone calls. The first was to Chippenham police station to see if there were any further developments and the second was to Bill Laidlow asking if it would be possible to meet up so that they could compare notes on this FORBOR outfit.

The first call yielded very little information, save for the fact that their door to door questioning had turned up an elderly lady who was out walking her dog on the night of the kidnap. She had spotted a largish yellow van parked well into the hedgerow close to the school gates. It could well have been a Transit from the description she was able to give. She also said that it had either tinted windows or maybe dark coloured panels painted on the side nearest to the road, so presumably on both sides. This tied in with the description of the van given to him by Bill Laidlow. The van which had been in the vicinity of the two explosions on the M5. It was all a bit tenuous but it was surprising how often these little fragments of information eventually slotted into place to form a clearer overall picture.

His second call to Bill Laidlow resulted in them arranging to meet over dinner at a restaurant just outside Cheltenham which was judged to be roughly the halfway point between the two of them. So having left his mobile number with Sergeant Bamford at Chippenham police station he set off and took a leisurely drive north towards Cheltenham, leaving his hotel about five o clock. He arrived at the restaurant before Laidlow and settled into a corner of the lounge with a large scotch. Ten minutes later Bill Laidlow arrived with his pipe clenched firmly between his teeth and still dressed in his comfortable old tweed jacket. When he had ordered a drink he turned round and saw that the Barnes was the only person sat in the lounge. He walked over and introduced himself.

'Bill Laidlow, you must be Inspector Barnes.'

Barnes stood up, a little taken aback. He had seen the older man walk in but hadn't taken much notice. He wasn't quite what he had been expecting when he had arranged to meet a Detective Superintendent of the Anti-Terrorism Squad.

'Good evening Sir,' he stammered,

'It's Harry by the way and thanks for agreeing to this meeting. Please sit down.' He passed Laidlow one of the large menus from the table,

'First things first Sir. I don't know about you but I'm ravenous.'

Puts me in mind of young Newman, Laidlow thought as he browsed through the extensive menu. Same smart suit, same manner. Keen as mustard no doubt and eager for promotion. A young girl in a very small black dress came and took their orders and asked if they would like another drink while they waited to be called through to the restaurant. They both said that they would and ten minutes later they were being led to their table.

Laidlow went through the events surrounding the explosions on the motorway in much more detail than he had over the phone, but concluded that they were no further forward with their investigations. Barnes in his turn went over the details of the kidnapping and the subsequent demands made by the group. They hadn't made much progress but had enjoyed an excellent meal, and as Barnes had remarked, as they left the restaurant, it always helped to put a face to a name.

They were both about to get into their respective cars when Barnes's mobile trilled out. Laidlow smirked to himself as he settled himself into the car. Bloody glad I don't have one of those contraptions he thought, your life is never your own. He had just turned the ignition key when Barnes came running over and tapped on the window. Laidlow wound it down and Barnes said,

I think there might have been a development Sir. That was Sergeant Bamford in Chippenham. It seems that some woman has rung in saying that she knows where Lady Samantha Simpkins is being held. I have got to take it seriously because, as you know, nothing about the kidnapping has been given to the media. The woman said that she would ring back later with the location.

* * * * * * *

Charlie had run into the farmhouse, tears of anger running down her face. She ran upstairs and started to throw her belongings into a large holdall, all the time muttering to herself,

Rotten bastard, was I not enough for him? I love him. WHY? Samantha only had to open her legs and he was there like a rat up a drain. Lousy cow. She can't resist can she. Like a bitch on heat.

She threw the holdall into the back of Norman's car and sped up the track towards the road, throwing up a spray of gravel as she went. She hadn't a clue where she was going , she just kept on driving round the narrow country lanes aimlessly. She was hurt. She felt let down, but most of all she was angry. She and Norman had seemed so right together, so natural and yet, there he was, at the first opportunity, it seemed, ready to screw Samantha at the drop of a hat, or should she say at the drop of her knickers. She pulled into the opening to a farm gate and sat there thinking about what she should do next.

She sat there for the best part of an hour, her mind in turmoil. She didn't even have Ginger to console her or to rationalise the situation. He was good at that, Ginger. His mind was so logical and precise. He never let emotions get in the way. . . she supposed that was his military training. Nevertheless she could really do with someone to talk to just now. She considered going down to her mother's house in Warminster, but dismissed it almost at once. She had only just brought herself to speak to her mother and their first meeting since her father's funeral had gone quite well. She didn't want to spoil that.

Then it came to her in a flash. *(Hell knows no fury like a woman scorned)* She would telephone the police and let them know where Samantha was being held. That would teach him, she thought. He was at the farm alone, except for Samantha that was, so the chances were that he would be arrested and that SHE would be returned to her husband where she belonged, the flighty cow. Any feelings of fondness that she'd had for her old school friend had immediately evaporated the minute she had seen Norman between her legs.

She had no idea how long she had been driving around the countryside, the clock in Norman's car wasn't working but, by the look of the sun sinking in the west, it must already be early evening. She started the car and drove through the country lanes until she came to the main road to Swindon. She drove into the town and found a row of public call boxes. She rang directory enquiries and got the number of the police station at Chippenham. That, she thought, would be the nearest one to where the kidnapping had taken place and presumably the investigations would be centred there. The phone started to ring out and after only three tones,

'Chippenham Police,' Sergeant Bamford's cheery voice boomed out, How can we help?'

'I would like to inform you of the whereabouts of Lady Samantha Simpkins, I believe that you are trying to trace her.'

'We might be,' said Bamford cautiously, trying to keep his tone non-committal.

'And who, may I ask, told you that we are looking for the lady, there's been nothing in the papers or on the television.'

Charlie suddenly became very nervous. How

could she have been so stupid. If she did tell them where Samantha was then she would surely implicate herself. Of course she could do it anonymously. She stammered into the phone,

'I'll ring you back later,' and she slammed down the receiver. She needed time to think. She walked quickly into the shopping precinct, the same precinct in which she had bought that delicious little green dress. God, that seemed centuries ago now. She found a little cafe, suddenly realising that she was very hungry. She ordered an omelette and a cup of coffee and sat there thinking while she ate.

Back at the police station in Chippenham George Bamford was climbing the flight of stairs which led to CID and to Detective Superintendent Fellows's office. His door was always open and Bamford marched straight in, they had known each other for too many years to stand on ceremony.

'Just had a strange call, Sir,' his tone was business-like despite their long friendship,

'Had a woman on saying that she knows the whereabouts of Lady Samantha Simpkins. I was beginning to think that the trail was going cold on that one.'

'So was I George, better get on to that Barnes fellow in London and let him know. See if he has got any further than we have.'

'As a matter of fact, Sir, he's not in London. He's in the area, Swindon to be precise. I've got his mobile phone number so I'll get on right away.'

'Thanks George. Keep me posted. I want to know the minute that woman rings back . . . that is, providing she does ring back.'

CHAPTER THIRTY ONE

Norman walked back from the barn towards the house swinging the empty tray and whistling as he went. As he rounded the corner he was surprised to see that his car was no longer parked outside the back door and he just assumed that Charlie had already set off for Cirencester on her shopping trip. He went into the kitchen to find the breakfast pots still on the table, shrugged and piled them into the dishwasher. He was still feeling on a high after his little escapade with Samantha and so, not surprisingly, there were no warning bells going off in his head.

He slipped on a jacket and went back to the barn to get the van out. He was tempted to go back to the tent, being as Charlie wasn't around, but thought better of it. He had to get up to Burford to make his telephone call to Sir Humphrey. He backed the van out and set off up the gravel track completely missing the deep wheel tracks which Charlie had made on her hasty departure from the farm.

At Burford he backed into a parking space on the right of the steep slope which is the main street. He walked to the local post office and went into the call box nearby.

The phone was picked up after three rings and a weary Sir Humphrey answered with his usual curt,

'Yes,'

'Sir Humphrey? Listen very carefully, I am not going to repeat myself. You have until tomorrow evening to persuade the government, through the auspices of your department, to make some statement regarding the banning of heavy goods vehicles on our roads. I think you know what will happen if such an announcement is not made,' and he slammed down the phone. He walked quickly up the steep street, got into the van and drove back up the hill and out of the town crossed the A40 and headed towards Lechlade and the farm beyond. He had no intention of hanging around after what Charlie had said about the amazingly quick response of the police in Marleborough

He turned into the driveway and was surprised to see that his car was still not by the back door. She must have put it straight into the barn, he thought as he stopped the van and jumped out.

'Hi, I'm back,' he called as he pushed open the kitchen door to be greeted by complete silence. Strange, he thought but then started to rationalise . . . she's probably decided to have her hair done or something. He pressed the button on the answer phone to see if she had left a message but the tape was blank.

'Well, not to worry,' he mumbled to himself as he set about finding something for his own and Samantha's lunch. Better not try anything though, when I take it down to her, he thought, Charlie could be back at any minute and if she happened to take his car down to the barn it could prove bloody embarrassing. He didn't know the half of it. After lunch he switched on the television switching aimlessly from one channel to another and then turned the set off again.

'My God, they put some bloody rubbish on during the daytime,' he was talking to himself again.

Teatime came and went and there was still no

sign of Charlie and Norman was starting to get really concerned now. What the hell could have happened? There had been no phone calls which was probably all to the good in one way . . . no news is good news. At least she hadn't been involved in an accident. Having said that, if she had been involved in an accident and was unconscious, the authorities wouldn't have a clue who to ring any way. He really didn't know what to think.

Charlie was still sitting in the cafe agonising over what she should do. Should she ring the police back and tell them where Samantha was being held or not. She loved Norman and had thought that he felt the same, but that was before this morning. This awful bloody morning. She sat staring at her empty coffee cup and thought of her recent doubts about what they had all become involved in. If she were to inform the police it would be an ideal way of extricating herself from a situation which was fast getting out of hand. There was nothing at the farm to connect her with the events of the past few days and she felt ninety nine per cent sure that Norman would not grass on her should he be arrested. Ginger, she was sure, was an expert at evading the law. He was perfectly capable of looking after himself. As it happened, she need not have concerned herself. Ginger Robson was, at that very moment, standing in a jungle clearing in Rwanda training members of the rebel army in the mysteries of the AK47 assault rifle. His urgent business had been an offer he couldn't refuse and within hours of leaving the farm he had been aboard a flight taking him to the continent of Africa.

The waitress appeared at Charlie's side,

'Have you finished with these?' she said indicating the empty cup and plate in front of her.

'Yes, I'm sorry. Are you waiting to close?' Charlie replied as if in a dream. She stood up from the table and headed for the door. The precinct was almost deserted now and walked aimlessly still deep in thought.

Finally she came to a decision. She wanted out and Norman must pay for his treachery. She walked towards the open area where the telephone kiosks were situated but as she rounded the last corner she stopped, as if to look in a shop window, turned and retraced her steps. There was a young police constable standing by the phones, surveying the various avenues which led to them.

She went quickly up to the car park and drove out. She had made another decision whilst going up in the lift. She would pay her mother another visit and make her phone call from somewhere along the way.

She joined the M4 just south of Swindon, headed east for a short distance and left at exit 16. She took the A3102 for Melksham. She decided that she would make her phone call there and then drive on to her mother's at Warminster. She chose a phone box on the outskirts of the town. It was an old traditional red one which was well away from prying eyes. She dialled the number of the police in Chippenham and it was answered almost immediately.

'Chippenham Police, Sergeant Bamford speaking,' answered the avuncular voice.

'Hello. I called earlier about the whereabouts of Lady Samantha Simpkins. You'll find her at Gore Farm near Castle Eaton,' she said in a faltering voice and slammed the receiver down at once. She almost ran to the car and drove off down the road towards the town centre. She was shaking quite badly and decided to pull over for a while. Why the on earth am I feeling so bloody guilty, she thought to herself. He shouldn't have done what he did, it was unforgivable. So why was she feeling like this? It was too late to do anything about it now and she started up the car, turned on the radio and set off on the final few miles to Warminster.

'Hello darling,' her mother greeted her at the door,

'What a lovely surprise. Are you by yourself? Is that nice young man not with you?'

'Oh mummy, I've done something awful,' and she burst into tears.

Her mother put her arm around her and led her into the lounge.

'Sit down darling and I'll put the kettle on, then you can tell me all about it. I'm sure it can't be that terrible.'

Three quarters of hour later her mother sat in stunned silence. Charlie had gone over the whole story from the minute she met Norman on a motorway slip road on that day which now seemed so long ago.

'I really don't know what to say Charlotte, I really don't.'

'Then don't say anything mummy, just hold me please and say that I can stay here with you until this whole ghastly thing blows over. I am absolutely sure that there is nothing to link me with either the bombings or the kidnap. I am convinced that if, I can just lie low for a week or so, everything will be alright.'

'But what about that poor young man who you have left to face the music, have you no feelings for him at all now? Surely it's not too late to phone him and at least give him a chance to get away and let them just find Samantha.'

'Yes you are right as usual mummy,' and she picked up the phone and dialled the number of the farm. It rang and rang for ages but there was no reply. Maybe he's down at the barn with Samantha she thought. Or worse still maybe he's moved her into the farmhouse. That thought fired her anger again and her mother noticed the muscles in her face suddenly tighten. She slammed down the phone and just sat there brooding.

'Aren't you going to try again,' her mother pleaded but she could see from the look on her face that she wasn't.

CHAPTER THIRTY TWO

The reason Norman hadn't answered the phone was that he had decided to drive up to Cirencester to see if he could find Charlie. He had been going crazy just sitting there wondering what had happened to her. He realised that it was probably a futile exercise but he just had to do something. Maybe she had broken down in one of the lanes miles from anywhere. Or possibly she had been to the hairdressers and had just lost track of time. It had never failed to amaze him just how long Jenny used to take having her hair done.

But of course the whole exercise had been a waste of time and he had not found her anywhere on the way to or from the town, despite the fact that he had tried a slightly different route on the way back. The light was starting to fail as he drove the last half mile to the farm and as he reached the brow of the hill overlooking it he passed a dark coloured saloon pulled over onto the verge. A bit early for a courting couple he thought as he drove past but a quick glance to the side revealed that there were two men in dark suits sat in the car and they were looking over the hawthorn hedge in the direction of the farm. Although he didn't know it, there was another car watching the entrance on the far side of the farm.

As soon as Sergeant Bamford had received Charlie's second call he contacted Barnes on his mobile. He had received the call just as he and Laidlow were leaving the restaurant and Laidlow had reluctantly borrowed the mobile gadget to contact Sergeant Newman. The two of them had organised a mobile incident room to be set up about half a mile from Gore Farm and within the hour all three of them were busy organising an operation which, hopefully, would lead to the release of the kidnapped woman.

The radio crackled and a monotone voice came over the speaker,

'Male I.C. one just entered the farm gateway

driving a yellow coloured Transit with dark coloured side panels.'

'That sounds familiar,' said Laidlow puffing on his old pipe which was already filling the caravan with a heavy pall of blue smoke.

'I think that we should wait until first light before making any move Sir,' said Barnes,

'I don't think that they are going anywhere in the foreseeable future and we don't know how many of them there are in the farmhouse and surrounding buildings. No point going in half-cocked and blundering about in the dark. We know that there are at least three people involved from the different voices we have recorded during the various phone calls. There is the Scot, there's the guy with the north-country accent and there's the woman, but there may well be more. I would prefer not to go in whilst it is dark not knowing how many we are up against and whether or not they are armed. We DO know that they are in possession of explosives and have the expertise to make good use of them. We know this from the two recent incidents on the M5.'

Laidlow nodded his agreement and then had a brief conversation with the men in the two cars who were keeping the farm under observation. His instructions were that one man from each car should try to get as near to the farm as they could without being observed and try to ascertain how many people were on the premises. He suggested that they do this after midnight or when the lights in the buildings went out.

Back in the farm Norman was feeling more than a little concerned about the two men he had just seen in the car. Where they on to him? Surely not. How could they be, they had been so careful, or so he thought. He was also very worried now about Charlie's disappearance. He was feeling very alone. First Ginger's hasty departure and now Charlie had gone missing. Things were going haywire and he didn't like it. He went out to the van and undid the secret compartment behind the seats. He took out the two items which Ginger had placed there and which they hoped they would never need to use. They were wrapped in heavy waxed brown paper and as he carried them into the house he felt a cold shiver run down his spine. It was the first time he had handled firearms of any sort since leaving the army.

He placed the packages on the kitchen table and as he opened the first one the, once familiar, smell of gun oil filled his nostrils. The gun was a Walther PK automatic, a weapon with which he was he was quite familiar. The second, and larger, of the packages contained an evil looking, snub nosed semi-automatic machine gun. Although Norman had never actually used this weapon before he was very aware of the devastating damage it could do. He could not really envisage himself pointing it at someone . . . not in peacetime. He wrapped the gun up again and hid it at the back of a cupboard under the kitchen sink.

Just after midnight the two men reported back to Laidlow that there was no way of telling how many people were in the farm. As far as they could tell there was actually only one that they could be sure of, but neither of them would have bet their next month's salary on that.

'OK, thanks. Just stay put and keep your eyes open', Laidlow said, the old pipe still clenched between his teeth although it was empty now, much to the relief of everyone else in the confined space of the caravan. He had organised an armed response team to report to him long before first light and all they could do now was wait.

Norman awoke with a start. He had lain on the double bed fully dressed and had finally gone to sleep despite the thoughts racing around in his head. He had come to the conclusion, just before he had finally succumbed to his exhaustion, that Charlie must have seen him with Samantha that morning in the barn. That was the only logical explanation for her disappearance and if that was the case she would be terribly hurt and upset. He was filled with a feeling of utter disgust at his behaviour and his thoughts returned yet again to the men in the car. Had she told the police? Were they were holding Samantha? He certainly couldn't blame her if she had. He deserved her contempt.

He went downstairs and made himself a drink and then he collected the package from the cupboard beneath the sink and the compact pair of binoculars from the dining room before returning to the bedroom. He carefully pulled one of the curtains aside and looked out across the field towards the road. Through the early morning mist he could see that the car was still there. He put the binoculars to his eyes and could make out the two men still sitting there.

As he placed the glasses on the window ledge something caught his attention behind the hedge which led down to the farm gates. It was the slightest of movements but he was sure that it wasn't a bird. It was too stealthy a movement for that. He picked up the glasses again and scanned the whole of the hedgerow. There it was again. This time he could see it. His hands started to shake and he strove to keep the binoculars steady. Barely visible above the top of the hedge he could just make out part of a navy blue baseball cap with a black and white chequered band. The sort of cap seen all too regularly on the television when the police were dealing with an armed siege situation or the like. He was in no doubt now. They knew and they were about to do something about it. At that moment Norman decided that he would not give up without a fight. Everything had gone wrong. He was on his own now and it was his own stupid bloody fault. He felt deep despair at that moment, after all, if he were to get himself killed, there would be no one to mourn his passing.

Laidlow, Barnes and Newman had moved

quite close to the gates of the farm now by Landrover and Laidlow stepped out with a bullhorn in his hand. The harsh crackly voice shattered the peace of rural early morning,

'Come out now with your hands raised. The place is completely surrounded.'

Norman buried his head in his hands, and then he snapped. He took the remote device for the explosives, switched it on and pressed the little red button. There was terrifying noise as all the charges blew at the same time.

Laidlow was thrown across the road into the wet undergrowth of the hedgerow. He was badly shaken but relatively unscathed. Barnes and Newman rushed across the road, gathered him up and bundled him into the Landrover which was quickly reversed down the road.

Norman was momentarily stunned by what he had done but then he thought, in for a penny in for a pound and he opened the bedroom window and fired off a few rounds from the evil looking machines gun.

'Right if that's the way they want it,' said Barnes,

'Get the guns as near to the house as possible and take out anyone who appears at any of the windows,' and picking up the bullhorn he continued,

'Send out the woman unharmed and then we can talk about your demands,' and in an aside to Newman, he added,

'In their bloody dreams!'

Norman had seen the movement of armed policemen through the gap in the curtains and he sank to the floor with his knees under his chin. He was scared and couldn't decide what to do. His family were dead, Charlie had left him, with good reason . . . God he hated that bitch in the barn. It was a great pity she wasn't here with him in the house. He was angry and frustrated enough to kill her and then take his own life. There was nothing to live for now and they would never take his demands seriously. He knew that now. Whatever made him think that he could change anything?

CHAPTER THIRTY THREE

Whilst the siege was in full swing at Gore Farm, Charlie had decided that she should get rid of Norman's car as soon as possible. She persuaded her mother to follow her down to Salisbury in her own car and, just before ten they both entered the large car park behind a supermarket not far from the cathedral. They decided to make a morning of it and walked down the narrow street and through the archway towards the grounds of the cathedral admiring the tallest steeple in the land as they went. After enjoying a quiet half hour or so inside the church they did some shopping and had lunch before returning to the car park. Charlie put a further four hour "Pay and Display" sticker on

Norman's car which would mean that it would be tea time or even the following morning before anyone started to take any notice of it.

They arrived home just after one and her mother turned on the television just in time for the local news. Charlie took a deep breath and swallowed hard as she saw the familiar surroundings of Gore Farm swarming with armed police. She had never visualised anything like this when she had turned Norman in. She was horrified and she sank into an armchair hugging one of the cushions. Her mother saw the look on her face but decided to say nothing for the time being. Charlotte had obviously realised what she had done and didn't need it rubbing in. She did what most people do in situations like that . . . she went to put the kettle on. A cup of tea. The great British panacea for every crisis.

Meanwhile back at the farm the armed response team was closed up and awaiting instructions. Samantha who had heard the explosion, albeit muffled by the insulating effect of all the bales surrounding her tent, sat on the edge of her bed wondering what on earth was happening. Was there some sort of rescue operation being mounted? Maybe, during the short time she had known him, she had severely underestimated Barnes and the resources which he could bring to bear. The thing which puzzled her most however was, how the hell had they found this God forsaken place so soon. Had her kidnappers made some terrible blunder or had someone spotted something quite by chance. Her mind was in turmoil. The very last thing which would have entered her mind was the fact that her old school chum Charlotte had been involved, first of all in the actual abduction and even more incredible the fact that she had been instrumental in bringing about her imminent release from captivity.

Bill Laidlow who had now recovered from the shock of being blown across the road earlier took hold of the bullhorn for one last attempt to coax out the kidnappers without having to resort to an armed assault.

'This is your last chance to release the woman and come out unarmed and with your hands held high above your heads,' the brittle distorted voice rang out, totally at odds with the peaceful surroundings.

Norman was still slumped beneath the

bedroom window, his head buried in his hands, battling with his mixed emotions. Should he just give up and face the music or should he try to fight it out or, and the third alternative made him break out in a sweat when he thought about it . . . merely turn the gun on himself and finish it there and then. That would probably be the best solution for everyone he thought morosely but then that strongest of all human instincts, self- preservation, kicked in and he decided to give himself up and face, probably a long term of imprisonment. He picked up the two weapons and made his way down the stairs and into the kitchen. As he passed the window he saw several men draw their assault rifles closer into their shoulders and stand totally alert. He carefully opened the kitchen door and stepped out into the porch throwing both weapons out and then he stood perfectly still. He knew the drill from his time in Northern Ireland. One of the armed policemen started walking slowly towards the door. He stopped about fifty yards short and started shouting,

Walk slowly out. Hands above your head,' and when Norman was well clear of the door he was ordered to,

'STOP WHERE YOU ARE! How many more are there inside,?'

'There's nobody else in there. I'm alone,' Norman's voice was very shaky and he was sweating profusely.

'RIGHT, DOWN ON THE GROUND,' screamed the Sergeant, reminiscent of his drill sergeants so long ago.

'Legs spread wide apart, arms behind you head,' and covered by four guns he went over and kicked Norman's feet, spreading his legs painfully whilst prodding his gun into the small of his back. He then replaced the gun with his knee and snapped his handcuffs roughly round his wrists. He dragged Norman roughly to his feet and, with his face close up to him shouted,

'Now where's the woman and no tricks,' and having said that he screamed to the four men who had been covering him,

'Get inside and clear the house. Check each room carefully for the woman.'

'She's not in the house,' said Norman nervously,

'She is in the barn at the bottom of the track there,' nodding with his head in the direction of the out buildings. A quarter of an hour later the

Sergeant spoke into his radio informing Laidlow that the house was now secure and that, according to the lone kidnapper, the woman was being held in the barn.

Laidlow and Barnes, together with four more armed men made their way cautiously down the track towards the building. It seemed hard to believe that there were not more people around the farm and as they approached the big double doors of the barn two of the armed men carefully pushed one side open then leapt inside, guns at the ready. The place seemed empty but all four gunmen approached the bales gingerly and rounded the corner of them one at a time pointing their guns in different directions as they went.

They surrounded the tent and as one of them entered the front flap the men on either side took out knives and slit the side panels from top to bottom. Samantha almost passed out as the rent appeared in the blue nylon fabric alongside her and an automatic rifle was poked through. Barnes walked into the tent and said quite calmly and business-like,

'Are you alright Maam,?'

Samantha stood up rather shakily, stepped

forward and threw her arms around the Inspector's neck,

'Oh, Harry, yes I'm alright. I've never been so pleased to see anyone in all my life,' and she continued to cling to him. Barnes looked over to where Laidlow and his Sergeant were standing and saw that Newman had a silly smirk on his face. Barnes, colouring slightly shouted,

'OK Sergeant, it's not a bloody peepshow. Go and tell the Inspector in charge of the armed team that they can stand down now . . . if that's alright with you Sir,' he said looking over to Laidlow.

When Charlie and her mother turned on the television for the local evening news they were horrified to see Norman laying spread-eagled on the dirt track with a burly policeman kneeling on his back, clamping handcuffs on him. The television crew had zoomed in on the action and Charlie could see the look of utter resignation on his face. She felt so sorry for him. How could she have done such a thing?

Then the cameras shifted. Barnes and two more men were escorting Samantha up the track from the barn to the police car which had somehow managed to get round the craters left by the explosions. She looked as though she was enjoying every single minute of it, smiling at the cameras and looking like a "million dollars" despite the loose fitting, slightly soiled overalls. She was basking in all the attention and Charlie felt a hatred welling up inside her, the like of which she had never experienced before.

Norman was being pushed roughly into the back of another car now, one of the plain clothes policemen pressing his head down as he went. He would be taken directly to Chippenham for extensive questioning before appearing before the town's Magistrates the following morning. The main thrust of the questioning would, of course, be aimed at finding out the whereabouts of the others who had been involved in the kidnap. There were definitely two more that they knew about, possibly more and the police would be very anxious to track them down, but they would get no help from Norman. He had already decided that. Nothing would get him to reveal the names or possible whereabouts of Charlie or Ginger.

Charlie sat there with tears streaming down her face.

'I must go to him mummy. He looked so

wretched, I can't bear it.'

'NO,' said her mother adamantly,

'No that is the last thing you should do. For God's sake Charlotte, just think it through. I am very sure, from what you have told me about that young man, that that's the last thing Norman would wish you to do. You can do nothing for him just now. All you would achieve by trying to see him would be to implicate yourself. Perhaps, in time, you could write to him but for the time being darling, I suggest you do nothing. If that sounds terribly selfish, then I'm sorry but I've only just got you back and I don't want to lose you again.'

EPILOGUE

Norman had been questioned until after midnight when the duty solicitor had insisted that he be given a break. He had told them absolutely nothing. He believed in the right to silence despite the new caution which stated that "It could harm his defence if he failed to say something that he might later rely on in court"

He had been returned to his cell and had cringed slightly as the heavy metal door was slammed when the custody Sergeant left. He lay on the blue plastic mattress on the bunk which occupied the wall opposite the door and stared up at the bare electric bulb shining starkly behind its wire grill. He was very tired but he could not sleep, there was so much racing around in his head. Why had he been such a bloody fool? He had let everyone down, including himself. Jenny certainly wouldn't thank him for what he had done, allegedly on her behalf. She had far too much common sense. She would be up there somewhere heaving that sigh of exasperation as she had done so often when he had done something stupid. He had let down Charlie who had given him so much. She had given him back his life after four terrible years in a self-imposed limbo and he had repaid her with betrayal, all for the sake of a ten minute romp with her old school friend. What sort of a lousy bastard had he turned into? Perhaps his decision to give himself up had been made out of an overwhelming need to be punished. He lay there punishing himself over and over again and almost looked forward to whatever sentence was handed down to him. God knows I deserve it he thought. He must have slept eventually. He was startled into consciousness again by the loud metallic sound of a key being inserted into the cell door.

'Breakfast!' and a surly young constable placed the plastic tray on the bunk beside him. He took hold of the mug of sweet milky tea and drank half of it in one swallow, but the sight of the greasy egg and the piece of bacon swimming in a pool of fat turned his stomach. He pushed the tray to one side despite the fact that he hadn't eaten for over twenty four hours.

He made a brief appearance before the Magistrates later in the morning when the charges were read out and he had said a subdued 'Yes,' when asked was his name Norman Edward Parker, and again when the clerk read out his address. He was remanded in police custody for seven days until investigations could be completed. A week later he was placed on remand to appear before Bristol Crown Court. Norman realised that this could be months away. Once, a long time ago, when he had been called for Jury service, the defendant in the case for which he had been selected, had been on remand for ten months before coming to trial.

Inspector Barnes had driven Lady Samantha directly to the house in Eaton Place so that she could be reunited with her husband as soon as possible. He had phoned Sir Humphrey as soon as she had been released and had persuaded Laidlow that he should do the debriefing in the comfort of her own home. There seemed no point in prolonging her ordeal by subjecting her to hours of questioning in a police station.

'I'm so very grateful to you Barnes,' Sir Humphrey was unashamedly wiping tears from his eyes as he said,

'It's so good to have you home my dear,' turning to Samantha.

'It's marvellous to be back darling and I promise that I'll not be such a bitch in future. I really do love you despite the awful way I treat you sometimes.'

Barnes left the room. He felt rather superfluous for the time being. The questioning could wait until later. They needed some time alone and he was most surprised that her Ladyship was still wearing the overalls she had worn during her captivity. A week ago, the first thing she would have done would have been to rush upstairs, take a shower then put on her make-up and one of her many little designer outfits. Maybe some good might come out of all this he thought as he wandered into the kitchen to make himself a cup of tea.

A month later in Bristol Prison, Norman received a letter. It was the first communication he'd had with the outside world since being sent there. It read.

Dear Norman,

I hope that one day you might be able to forgive me for what I have done to you. It was a spiteful thing to do and there isn't a day goes by when I don't regret it bitterly. I was hurting so much after seeing you with HER, I loved, you so much. My dearest hope is that, one day we might be able to see each other again and at least be good friends. I will of course understand if you never want anything to do with me again.

All my love,
Charlie.

The questioning of Samantha, when it finally took place, revealed not a single thing that they didn't already know. Samantha had been blindfolded whenever any of the kidnappers were around. She could only verify what they already knew about their accents, so it seemed likely that Parker would be the only one charged and would carry the can alone.

When the case finally came to court Charlie was sat in the public gallery wearing a plain grey jersey dress and her blonde hair was almost shoulder length now. As Norman was led into the dock he looked around the courtroom and caught sight of her on the back row. He looked at her and she smiled that special smile and he immediately regretted the cool, indifferent content of the short note he had sent in reply to her letter. He wished now that he could just go over and hug her and tell her that everything was alright but he was standing between two burly warders.

The clerk of the court banged his gavel and called,

'The court be upstanding,' and accompanied by a loud shuffling of feet the judge entered and sat down.

The charges were read and Norman was asked,

'How do you plead, Guilty or not guilty" and the trial got underway. After a day and a half of examination and cross examination of witnesses and police experts the Jury were sent out to consider their verdict. Charlie sat in the cafeteria staring at her cup of cold coffee praying as she had never prayed before that the sentence would be a light one. It was a pretty forlorn hope however. The establishment were very keen to make an example in this case if only to discourage any further attempts to abduct the relatives of prominent figures.

Everyone was called back into the courtroom

and the jury filed back into their seats.

'Have you reached a verdict on which you all agree?'

'We have.'

'On the charge of causing the said explosions how do you find the defendant, guilty or not guilty?'

'Guilty"!

'And on the charge of kidnap how do you find the defendant, guilty or not guilty?'

'Guilty!'

Norman stood expressionless in the dock thinking, my future lies in the hands of that desiccated old fart and he's obviously completely out of touch with the real world. The judge slowly removed his spectacles and started into a long discourse on the seriousness of the offences and how our public figures and their relations should be protected from the likes of Norman Parker. Of course that was exactly what one would expect him to say, he being a prominent figure and him having a vested interest so to speak. The last thing he wanted was for his cosseted privileged lifestyle to be threatened in any way. He finally finished his droning by telling the court that he would pass sentence in seven days following psychiatric reports on the prisoner.

Norman Parker was sentenced to fifteen years for the kidnap and ten years for the explosions, the sentences to run concurrently. With a bit of luck and if he kept his nose clean Norman, according to his brief, could be out in eight.

Charlie and her mother heard of the sentence which Norman had been given on the early evening news and Charlie decided there and then, that no matter where he served his time, she would visit him as often as she could.

Two months later when Norman was reading the first of his morning newspapers, The Guardian, he spotted a small article on page four of the paper. It was no more than three column inches but he couldn't help but smile at the irony of it. It told of an American company which was to start up the first new Railway Wagon company to be formed in Britain this century. They were to build new freight wagons at the old Railway Works in York which would service the ever increasing rail freight services which were now thriving thanks to the Channel Tunnel.

He patted his latest letter from Charlie in his

breast pocket. He would read it again after supper tonight and write a reply. The letters were all that were keeping him going. They were the only relief in the grinding daily boredom which he would have to endure for the next eight years or so. He would tell her about the little article he had just read and he knew that she would smile a wry smile just as he had done at the absolute irony of it.

As he read the letter again later that evening he was filled with anticipation. Charlie had managed, at last, to obtain a visiting pass and would be coming on Thursday. He could now see a glimmer of light at the end of the tunnel even though it was a bloody long tunnel.

* * * * * * *